AF505667

EVIL LIVES AMONG US

J L Lara

It is a scary thought that there are people out there pretending to be human beings.

EVIL LIVES AMONG US

Copyright © 2021 by J. L. Lara
All rights reserved

This eBook is licensed for your personal enjoyment only. No part of this book may be reproduced or transmitted in any form or by any electronic or mechanical means, including information storage and retrieval systems, without written permission from the author.

This book is a work of fiction. All names, characters, places, and incidents are the product of the author's imagination or are used fictitiously. Any resemblance to actual persons, living or dead, events or locales, is coincidental.

OTHER BOOKS BY THE AUTHOR – AVAILABLE ON GOODREADS AND AMAZON

A Hard Reset
Worst Of Days
Hunt, Trap, and Kill – A Hannah Sterling Mystery - Book 1
Murder and Mayhem in West Palm Beach – A Hannah Sterling Mystery – Book 2
Thrill Of The Hunt – A Hannah Sterling Mystery – Book 3
The Discovery Of Bones – A Hannah Sterling Mystery – Book 4
The Black River Killer
Body Count – A Sheriff Katy Bell/Navaho Mystery
The Baking Club Murders – Pecan Pie
Fresh Kill – A Detective Jada Jameson Novel
Last Breath
Deadly Desires
The Holiday Killer
The Traveler
Punishment
Killer Among Us
First To Live

DEDICATION

As always, to my wife for her support. To my family and friends for their encouragement.

TABLE OF CONTENTS

Chapter 1

This evening started off like any other for Deputy Jimmy Dearing. He only had two hours left on his shift when the call came in for a woman in distress on Arkansas Route 298. Her vehicle had broken down on that long dark stretch and she was afraid, so she had dialed 911 instead of calling for a tow truck and having a long wait. Deputy Dearing was not that far away, so he took the call and responded as the distant flashes of lightning began to appear over the Ouachita River. He worked out of the Hot Springs Village Sheriff's sub-station, so Route 298 was one of his regular areas to patrol.

He figured that if he hurried and got the lady the help she needed real quick he could have her back in Hot Springs Village in time for his shift to end. He was going on a ten day vacation beginning tomorrow and still had some last minute packing to do, so he turned his light bar on and stepped on the accelerator. It had been threatening to rain for the past two hours, and the farther west he headed on Route 298, the more brilliant the flashes of lightning became. Four miles later he saw the dim four way flashers on the back of a car and assumed that it was the woman who had called in. As he drew close to her vehicle he slowed and began to look for her as light rain began falling on his windshield.

He stopped just behind her car and got out of his patrol car, then walked to the driver side of the vehicle and looked in. It was empty. He yelled out "Garland County Sheriff Department, hello!" There was no response as the rain began getting a little thicker, so he walked around the vehicle continuing to call out. Maybe some vehicle came by ahead of him and she hopped a ride with them he thought. One more look inside the vehicle and that thought left him immediately as soon as he saw a purse on the passenger seat. He looked around again, then he opened the door and took a look inside the purse. He found the driver's license and the name matched the description of the woman that had called in.

Confused as how this woman could have left her purse behind, he decided to take a walk around the vehicle. He knew that there were rattle snakes out here, as well as wild animals, and it was possible that the woman decided to head into the brush to go to the bathroom and somehow encountered one of those creatures. He grabbed his flashlight and began to search as he now called out to her by her name, Amanda Webb. The rain showed no mercy now as it began coming down harder, limiting his visibility. A few more minutes of searching did not produce anything, and there were no signs that anyone had walked out there anyway, so he decided to head back to the car and search in front of the vehicle.

It only took a few minutes for him to see some fresh tire tracks about twenty yards in front of her car, and footprints leading back to her car, so he assumed that someone had stopped and helped her. He ran back to his unit and called it in, keeping her purse to show that he had come to offer assistance. He told the dispatcher about the tire tracks and footprints, then asked them to call ahead to the town of Story, as it was the only area that had a few service stations. He knew that everything was closed for the night, so he figured that she would have gone there, then had someone pick her up. It baffled him as to why she had not called to report that she had caught a ride so that there would not have been a need to dispatch a deputy, but he knew how people were.

Once he arrived back at the sub-station he turned her purse in to dispatch, filled out his report, then hung out there until his shift ended. Even though it was pouring outside, as he went home for the night all that he could think about was that vacation coming up in the morning.

The white van cruised down Route 298, and as it headed west he saw the streaks of lightning up ahead. The rain was about to arrive, and he wanted to make it home before it did. Another mile down the road he spotted the flashers on a vehicle that had pulled off the road and he began to slow down. He went slowly past it and smiled as he saw a lone woman sitting inside. This was a pleasant find and surprise for him, so he pulled ahead and stopped the van. He stuffed his revolver behind his back, straightened his hair, then got out of the vehicle, spitting a large chaw of tobacco on the ground as he started walking towards the car.

He looked in all directions but did not see anyone else, so he smiled as he drew close to the car then stopped. He bent slightly and waived, and he could smell the rain in the air. It was coming anytime now. The woman appeared to be speaking on her cell phone, so he stood there smiling and waving slowly at her. She finally stopped speaking and he called out to her, "Is everything alright Maam? Do you need some help?" The woman smiled back weakly and waived him off as she turned her head to indicate that she did not want any help. He was not going to leave here without her, so he stepped closer to the car and said, "Did you hear me Maam? I asked if you needed assistance? I am a mechanic and I have my tools in the van. I would be happy to help you and you can stay in the car if you prefer, it's starting to rain now."

He saw the hesitation, and he knew that he had her now. He saw the door open slightly and figured that the car had no power so she could not open her window. He stayed put and smiled, then said, "Honestly, I can help you if you let me. I can get your car running for you before the rain gets harder." He pointed to the skies behind him just as more streaks of lightning flashed and a loud rolling thunder boomed ahead of them. The woman looked at it, then said, "Thank you sir, but I already called 911. They are sending a deputy to help." He nodded then said, "That is fine Maam, but I may be able to get this running for you. If you lost power you may just have a dead battery. I have a spare that I can put in your car for free. It will only take me five minutes if you allow me. Like I said, feel free to remain in your vehicle even though it has to be very hot and stuffy in there."

She smiled and nodded, then said, "OK thank you very much.

I will pay you for the battery though." He said, "No need to, it's only a spare and I just could not take your money. How about you reach under there and pop the hood for me." She nodded and tried to find the handle, but in the dark she struggled to find it. He was now standing just outside her window, so he said, "Maam, please allow me to pop the hood. I want to get that battery in there before the rain gets worse, I'm already getting wet out here." He made sure to give her his biggest smile then, and she nodded as she moved back on her seat. He grabbed the door and slowly pulled it open, then he bent down as if he was going to pop the hood open when he suddenly threw a quick upper cut punch that caught her under her chin, snapping her head back against the seat back.

In an instant she was out like a light, so he slid his hands under her legs and lifted her out of the vehicle, closed the door with his foot, and began walking hurriedly to his van with her. Once he had her secured in the back of the van with zip ties on her wrists and ankles and duct tape over her mouth, he punched the accelerator and got back on the pavement as the rain began to come down steadily. He glanced back in his rearview mirror for any sign of the deputy, then he smiled when he did not see anything but pitch black in his mirror. He stepped on the accelerator and watched the speedometer climb to seventy as the van quickly departed from the scene. Feeling like he had just struck gold, he began to whistle as he thought about his find. What luck he had! To find a beautiful young woman out in the middle of nowhere with no one around was a real treat. He hadn't even thought about taking a woman captive before, but he just couldn't let an opportunity like that pass by. He felt thrilled now and decided that he would place her in the spare bedroom, but he had some changes to make to it now. The heavy rain caused him to slow down because visibility was getting worse, and now he heard the constant cranking noise of the windshield wipers as they struggled to sweep the constant pounding on the glass from the rain storm.

A few miles later he turned south on the dirt road and slowed down so that the old van would not get caught in one of the large ruts or puddles and cut out on him. The rain began to come down harder and lightning lit up the night as booming bursts of thunder blanketed the area all around him. He still had two more miles to go and did not want to have any problems on the road now. Feeling really excited, he slapped the dash and let out a shout of joy as the adrenaline coursed through his veins. The woman was still out cold in the back of the van, and she may not wake up until he reached home, but now she belonged to him and no one had seen a thing.

Home was a fifty three acre farm that had belonged to his father before he died. He and his brother inherited the land afterwards and had stayed on, catching fish and selling them for a living until his brother got caught by police and charged with rape and kidnapping of a young girl that was only seventeen years old. His brother received a long prison sentence for his crimes, and now he alone sold the fish he caught to local restaurants in the nearby towns to make a living. The family had been very fortunate to have a creek running on their property that fed into the large body of water called the Ouachita River. They had lived alone for years until one day his brother brought a woman home he had taken from a restaurant parking lot without realizing that there were security cameras capturing his every move.

He himself was not at home at the time because he was out setting trot lines, but once he made it home, he saw that his entire small ranch was completely surrounded by Sheriff deputies, then he saw the woman coming out of his home being escorted by two deputies. He did not know what was happening until he saw two more deputies bringing his brother out handcuffed. He had remained hidden as he watched the scene unfold, then he decided to stay away from the courtroom when his brother was sentenced for fear of going to jail with him. As it turned out, his brother had since died in prison months later due to a fight he had picked with one of the inmates. Since that day he had lived alone until he had encountered the woman on the road. Now he would have her all to himself, knowing that no one had seen him taking her, and he would not be alone any more.

He finally saw the gate up ahead and stopped to unlock it. Once he pulled the van through he locked the gate once again and headed to the house. After parking the van and carrying her into the house, he took her to the back bedroom and placed her on the bed, placed another zip tie from her wrists to the bed frame, then went to his shed and gathered some supplies as the intensity of the storm increased. He had to make sure that she was not able to escape, and that no one could hear her if they happened to get close to the house. He felt secure knowing that no one knew that this property even existed, and it had been three years since the law had taken his brother away, so as far as they were concerned, this property was now abandoned.

He had kept out of trouble, not even getting so much as a parking violation, and he knew that the law would never even suspect him of taking that woman. He now began boarding up the only window in the bedroom after stuffing the pink insulation between the boards, then he began securing more insulation to cover every inch of wall before adding more pieces of wood on top of it. Confident that he had made the room a lot more soundproofed, he drilled two holes into the concrete block and attached large steel plates, securing them with lag bolts. He was going to attach two large chains to them to keep her secure. He heard the woman stirring as she lay on the bed and looked over at her. She finally turned to look at him, then she tried to sit up on the bed until she realized that she had been tied down.

He heard her trying to scream but the gag he had placed on her mouth prevented anything but muffled sounds from coming out, then he saw the tears begin to flow from her eyes once she realized what had happened to her. Knowing that she wasn't going anywhere, he turned away and resumed securing the chains to the steel plates, then he placed steel clamps at each end of the chain. One would go around her ankle and the other on one of her wrists. The chains were not too heavy, but they were strong enough so that she would never be able to break them. He could leave her chained up during the time he went to collect his fish and took them to sell and not need to worry that she could escape. Living way out here in this remote location ensured that no one would ever be able to find her.

He stood after he gathered his tools and looked down at her, then said, "I'm fixing the room real nice for you so that you have everything you need to be comfortable. You're gonna be living here from now on, so the quicker you realize and accept that, the better off it's gonna be for you. I'll be right back." He left the room and put his tools back in the shed, then he brought out the port-a-potty that he used when he and his brother would camp out on a hunting trip. He would keep it in her room so that she would not have to leave it to use the bathroom.

Keeping her secured in the room would make everything easier for him and she would never be able to look for a way out. He had decided that he would provide things for her to keep her entertained, and that he would make sure she had plenty to eat and drink, so he figured that she would eventually get used to her surroundings and accept her fate. He knew that he was going to have to break her, but he was ready to do whatever it took in order to make her submissive to him.

The bedroom had a small twin bed and a small night stand, plus one lamp and the overhead light. The small closet had a few of his things in it that he had to remove, then the room would be all hers. Eventually he would need to buy her some clothing and underwear as well as some female stuff as he called it, but for now all that she needed would be provided. He had a small television in the bedroom that he never used, so he would place that in her room, as well as an old radio he had kept in the shed. He would go to the store tomorrow and buy some magazines and books for her too, as well as some snacks, but he wanted to know what she liked, and he had to explain the rules to her so that she understood what he expected from her. For now he would not force himself on her, but he would make sure that she knew that she wasn't here just to keep him company.

Chapter 2

Deputy April Sanders read the report from last night after having received a phone call from the parents of Amanda Webb. She had seen the contents in the purse, and now held the driver's license in her hand that identified the purse as that belonging to Amanda. She picked up the receiver and dialed Deputy Dearing, hoping to catch him before he took off for his vacation.

Dearing answered on the second ring, and April said, "Jimmy, this is April. Hey, I read your report about the woman on Route 298 last night, Amanda Webb." He said, "Oh, did someone finally find out where she went to?" April said, "No, not yet. Her parents called to report her missing. Amanda went out to meet a friend at seven last night and eat at a pizza joint in Hot Springs Village. She never came home last night and they have not heard from her. I have a couple of questions for you real quick." He said, "Sure, what do you need to know?" April said, "According to your report, you first approached the vehicle and did not see anyone around, then you searched around it as you identified yourself loudly, correct?"

Jimmy said, "That's right, and there was no response at that time." April said, "Then you went back to the vehicle and did a more thorough look inside of it. That was when you saw her purse, pulled it out, and looked up her ID." He said, "That is correct. I called out to her, then I walked to the front of the vehicle. That was when I saw tire tracks and foot prints. I assumed that someone had come along and that she had caught a ride with them." April said, "Knowing that she had dialed 911, did you search for her cell phone?" There was silence on the line, then he said, "I ah, I didn't see one, just the purse on the front passenger seat, I guess I figured that she must have taken it with her, but I really didn't even think about it at the time."

April said, "Any signs of a struggle at all?" Now Jimmy became worried, and said, "No, like I said, all I saw was the tire marks ahead of her car maybe twenty yards or so, and it was raining real hard by then. I called it in and left the scene after that. Do you think that someone took her April?" She said, "Not sure yet, I need to get out to her vehicle right away and check. Keep your phone handy in case I have some more questions please." He said, "Do you need me to post pone my vacation?" April did not see a need for that, so she told him to enjoy his time off but to keep his phone handy, then she told her dispatcher where she was headed, and took off.

Deputy April Sanders was a seven year veteran of law enforcement, having spent all of her law career as a deputy with the Garland County Sheriff's Department. She was a local that had been born and raised in Hot Springs, Arkansas, and had attended a community college for two years before transferring to the University of Arkansas in order to get her degree in criminology before accepting a position with the Garland County Sheriff's Department. She had recently taken and passed the exam to become a detective and was awaiting the promotion to come through at any time. For now she resumed her deputy duties and began her shift that day the same way she always did, by reading the reports from the last shift.

Travelling west on Route 298, it only took her thirty minutes to arrive at the car that she suspected belonged to Amanda Webb. She pulled in behind it and got out, then walked up to it and peered inside. There were no signs of foul play that she could see, and she saw footprints all around the driver's side of the vehicle. There were two different sets of prints, so she figured one belonged to her deputy, Jimmy Dearing. She instantly recognized which set was from Jimmy's boots since she wore the same boots herself, but it was the other set that she was interested in. They lead to the front of the vehicle, so she began to follow them as she kept to the pavement.

Just as Deputy Dearing had reported, approximately twenty yards ahead there were a set of tire marks on the side of the road, and that was where the footprints she was following ended. She began walking back to the car looking closely at the footprints and noticed that they were not as deep as the ones coming back to the tire prints.

Next she walked on the passenger side of the car and again noticed her own deputy's footprints, but none other. She saw where, like his report had stated, he had walked off to the side of the road, and managed to find his prints in the brush as he looked around for her. She did not see anything out of place here, no broken or bent branches, nothing laying on the ground, so she assumed that April had not come this way. Now she headed back to her car and, wearing her gloves, opened the rear door and looked inside. The back seat was empty, and there was no sign that anyone had been back there, so she closed the door and opened the front passenger door.

One quick look on top of the empty seat, then she opened the glove compartment. Other than a small box of Kleenex, a small bottle of hand sanitizer, the only other items in there were the vehicle owner's manual, the car registration, and an insurance card. All with Amanda's name and address on it. She pulled the visor down and saw that it was empty, then she bent down and looked under the seat. Although there was nothing under it, she saw the corner of what appeared to be a cell phone as it hung down, stuck in between the seat and center console. She rose up slowly and looked, then she saw the cell phone. It looked like April had stuck it in between the seat and center console on purpose, so she decided to leave it there until her crime scene team could check it for prints.

April repeated the same process on the driver's side of the car, but there was nothing there that told her anything. She went back to her patrol car and called for her crime scene unit, then she waited for them to arrive to make sure that no one would come by and disturb the scene. As she waited for her team to arrive she began thinking about last night's events. From what it appeared to her so far, Amanda's car had broken down on the side of the road. It was night, and this road has no lights on it since it is out in the country side. Amanda must have felt fear being out here all alone, so she dialed 911 and waited. The weather turned foul and it rained heavily as she waited alone, then another vehicle happened by and stopped just ahead of her car.

She looked ahead again to gain a better perspective of the distance, then it struck her that the vehicle had parked a ways away. Maybe in order not to frighten her or maybe because it was traveling fast and by the time it stopped it was about twenty yards away. Or possibly so that she could not read the license plate from that distance in the dark, stormy night. That vehicle's owner walked back to her car, which meant that she must have spoken with them. There was no sign of a struggle at all, but the footprints going back to the vehicle seemed heavier, much heavier, than the ones coming from the vehicle to her car. That meant that she may have been carried back to the vehicle. Still, there were no signs of a struggle at all, and only one set of prints other than the ones from her deputy.

Maybe she was not conscious when she was taken back to the vehicle parked in front of hers she thought. She knew that it was possible her cell phone would prove to be helpful, but she had to wait for the crime scene unit to process it first. She wanted to see who she had called besides having dialed 911, and she wanted to see if Amanda had taken any pictures with her cell. Hopefully the cell phone would provide her some new evidence and her crime scene people would be able to identify the tire marks from the vehicle that, in her view, had stopped to offer assistance.

According to her parents, Amanda was coming home from Hot Springs Village after meeting a friend for pizza at a restaurant called Charlie's Pizza. She would go there next and see if the store had video she could take a look at. She had also learned the name, address, and phone number of the friend that Amanda had met at the pizza place, so she would make sure to bring them in for questioning once she returned to the sub-station or possibly pay him a visit in person at his residence.

Twenty five minutes later her crime unit arrived, and April showed them the tire and foot prints, then pointed out the location of the cell phone to them. She waited for them to finish before calling her dispatcher to let them know that she was on the way to the pizza place, then she made sure that the crime scene unit had Amanda's car taken back to their lab before she left. Something about those tire marks and the heavier foot prints did not seem right to her, and she suspected foul play as she thought about the events there last night. She hoped that if someone had taken her last night they would keep her alive until she was able to determine who had stopped there.

She recalled that a few years ago there was a young woman kidnapped around there and, because of video evidence from a local restaurant, they had been able to find her and arrest the man responsible for the crime. She would need to look up that arrest to make sure that the man responsible for the crime was still behind bars. April lit up her light bar even though traffic on Route 298 was light. She wanted to get to the pizza store as quickly as possible so that she could also make a stop where Amanda's friend lived to speak with him.

It took about forty minutes for her to reach Charlie's Pizza on N State Hwy 7, then she asked for the store manager or owner as soon as she walked in. She noticed that there were two cameras inside the store and one outside in the side parking lot. Charles Smith smiled at her while he introduced himself, then she told him that she wanted to take a look at the video tape from last night in order to find out if a woman she was looking for had frequented the store. Charlie was very friendly to her and led her back to his office, then he began playing the tape, starting from six thirty last evening. He brought April a slice of pizza and a cold coke, and she thanked him for it as she began her search of the parking lot first.

She saw Amanda's car appear at five minutes to seven last night, and, at the same time, a silver Ford F150 came into the lot and parked beside her car. She watched a young man get out, walk over to her and hug her, then they kissed gently on the lips, held hands, and went inside the restaurant. The boyfriend. She wrote the license plate of the truck down as well as a brief description of it, then she focused on the video from inside the restaurant. She watched the tape closely for the next hour as the young couple had pizza and cokes, holding each other's hands at times, and laughing most of the time. Everything appeared normal to her, and it seemed that the two young people were just out on a date.

She noticed the sky had turned dark and wrote the time down from the video when the young couple stood, left a tip on the table, then went out to their vehicles. Now she looked closely as they leaned on her car, kissing softly and talking for the next ten minutes, then she watched as the young man stood back and made sure that Amanda got into her car. He waited until she had pulled away and got back on the road before he got into his truck, left the parking lot, then made a turn in the opposite direction. There had not been anyone in the parking lot at that time that had been watching the couple, and she had not seen any other vehicle leave the parking lot at the same time and begin following her car.

April asked the owner, Charlie, for a copy of the tape before she left the store, then she looked at the rest of the stores on N State Hwy 7 as she headed back towards Route 298. She listed the store names and called dispatch to ask her Sergeant for a court order she knew she would need in order to get video footage from them. She listed each store for him, then decided that she would send one of her deputies to those stores to collect their tapes as soon as she received the court order.

It was time now to take a ride and pay a visit to the young man that had shared a meal with Amanda last evening, twenty year old Ray Horton. According to Amanda's parents, the two had been dating for several months, having met in class at the community college. Ray lived in Hot Springs Village with his parents still while he attended the college.

April did not call ahead and hoped that he was at home. It only took ten minutes for her to arrive at his address, then she was let in by his startled father as soon as she asked to speak with his son. Ray appeared moments later wiping his hands with a rag. He explained that he was changing the oil in his truck in the garage, so April waited for him to wash up before asking him to sit. Both his mother and father asked to be in the living room with them while she spoke with their son. She was not certain if Amanda's family had called him or not, so she began by asking that question.

Ray immediately appeared surprised when she asked about Amanda, and said, "No, I haven't heard from her parents at all. Is everything alright Deputy Sanchez?" April said, "It seems that Amanda did not come home last night." She saw his mouth open wide as he said, "Oh my God!" What happened?" He sat next to his parents on the couch right away and his mother placed her arm around his shoulder. He seemed to be truly surprised to April, so she said, "I viewed video from Charlie's Pizza place and I saw that you met her there to eat last evening." Ray nodded and said, "Yes, that's right. We met there at around seven and ate, then I watched her get into her car. I waited til she was back on the road before I left to come home. What happened to her? Hasn't her family heard from her at all?"

April said, "No they have not Ray. I was hoping you knew if she maybe went to see anyone else after she left you last evening." He said, "No, she told me that she wanted to get home before the storm hit. She told me that it would take her an hour to get home from there, so I told her to be careful and I left. Oh my God, Amanda!" April saw tears coming from his eyes now, then his father said, "Deputy Sanchez, we can vouch that ray was back here at a little after eight last evening, and that he stayed home last night after that. He did not want to be caught in the storm either."

April said, "Ray, do you know if Amanda had any problems at home or if anyone was mad or upset with her?" His voice cracking now, Ray said, "Oh no, not Amanda. She is the sweetest person you could know. Anyone that meets her likes her because she is real friendly and outgoing. She always told me that she got along real good with her family. Please officer, find her." April said, "That is exactly what I am trying to do Ray. I need to find out who her friends are and speak with each one of them.

Can you give me a list of anyone that you know of who knows Amanda?" He stood and left the room, then his father said, "Tell me Deputy Sanchez, what do you know so far."

April told him about finding the car abandoned on the road but nothing else. She asked some basic information about their son, age, how long he had known Amanda, and how well they got along. She would not reveal any information to them while she investigated the case. Ray returned moments later with a list that had two names, and both were females. He said, "These are the two girls that she hangs out with from school. We both attend the community college in Hot Springs and have classes together. I only know their names and phone numbers and not where they live." She assured the family that she would do everything possible to find Amanda, thanked them for their time and asked Ray not to leave the area unless she was made aware first. She headed back to her office for the day to plan her next move. She would go over the video footage from the other stores in the area once she had them, but her next move was to speak with her parents personally and learn everything that she could about Amanda. She still felt that something had gone horribly wrong at the scene of her abandoned car, and she would know in the morning once she got the report from her crime scene unit.

She would make the call to the two friends to find out what they knew and if they knew if Amanda had any problems with anyone at the school, but that could wait until the morning. She thought about Amanda's cell phone again and could not wait to see what her team had found on it. Since it was near her shift time to end she decided to call it a day and she headed home, thinking about Amanda and praying that she was not in any harm. No matter what, she had to find out what had happened to her. She did not suspect that Amanda had run away from home, but she had to talk with her parents first to determine if that thought was correct.

Chapter 3

Amanda's tears had dried up after her kidnapper finally left her room. He had been back a few times and she had feared that he was going to rape her. Why else would he have kidnapped her she thought. She wished that she had been awake when she had arrived here, wherever here was, but as of right now she had no idea where she was being kept and she feared for her life.

As she thought about her situation now, she knew that she had failed to do what her father had told her to do, and that was to never trust any strangers, never, under any circumstances. She had fallen for his trick and had actually opened her car door, then she remembered him reaching in to pop the hood open after promising her that he was going to put a new battery in her car. Why had she believed him? She tried to remember what had happened once he reached inside the car, but for now she could not. Her head was sore and her chin hurt, so maybe he had hit her and knocked her out. There was no mirror in the room for her to look at herself, but when she pressed gently on her chin she felt a bit of pain.

He must have hit her hard and so quick that she never saw it coming. She had cried for a while as he worked on the room and she watched him put insulation on the walls then cover the window so that the room would be sound proofed and sealed from the outside, and it scared her when she thought that he was going to hurt her and did not want anyone to hear her screams. Once he had finished and returned he placed two chains on her. One on her ankle and the other on her wrist. They were long enough so that she could stand and walk around the room, and they made noise when she did. He had removed her gag and zip ties, then he brought in a small plastic toilet for her to use but forgot to bring her toilet paper and a way to wash her hands.

He did not appear to be very intelligent to her, but he was big and strong. He was over six feet tall and muscular, and had not shaved in a very long time. His beard was unkept just like his hair, and he smelled like fish to her. He was trying to be nice to her as he told her that he was going to bring a radio and a television into the room, then he told her that he would get her books and magazines to look at, as well as something to drink and some snacks. This really frightened her because that meant that he planned on keeping her there for a long time. It was the last visit from him that really frightened her as he went over some rules that he expected her to abide by.

She could not forget his rules, the first being that she was not to fight him in any way or he would beat her. She was not to scream or try to get away or he would punish her severely. Then he told her that at some point soon he would expect her to be cooperative when he came for her for sex. That thought brought more tears to her eyes now as she tried to think of how she could talk him out of it or maybe find her way out of this place. That guy did not seem normal to her and she feared that if she did not do as he said he would hurt her, or worse, he would kill her. Her thoughts turned to her family and to her boyfriend, Ray, and she knew that they would all be very worried about her. Somehow she was going to have to figure out a way to get away from this place or she feared that something really bad could end up happening to her. She hoped that the police would find her real soon, but she also knew that they may never find her, and that thought made her feel really sad.

That night was very difficult for her to get any rest. She could not hear a sound outside her door, and when she turned the television on all the she could get were two local channels, and the screen images on them both were very poor, most of the time they looked like snowy screens. She tried the radio also to see if she could hear any news about herself, but again she was only able to get a couple of stations that seemed like they were thousands of miles away as the voices went in and out, and one was in Spanish. She cried off and on as she thought about her situation, and she prayed a lot for herself and for her family. Finally she succumbed to some sleep and finally found a bit of peace in her head.

Deputy Sanchez was at the station early the next morning, and after filling her cup with hot coffee, she went to her desk and began compiling a list of things that she had to do. She knew that she would receive a report from her crime scene team concerning Amanda's car, possible finger prints and DNA, her cell phone, and hopefully the tire marks and footprints. She listed those on her paper, then added the names and phone numbers of the two women that were her friends from college. She decided to send a deputy to visit her boyfriend Ray and ask him to volunteer to give them his finger prints and a DNA sample. She felt that he would cooperate, and as of now considered him to be a person of interest only and not a suspect for now.

She listed the names of the other businesses in the area where she had requested a court order for their video tapes from, then she listed Amanda's address on her notes so that she could go and speak with her parents. She knew that they would want to know what progress she had made on her case so far, and she did not blame them, but there wasn't going to be much that she could tell them as of now. Until she cleared her parents of any foul play, she could not reveal any information to them about the case. She picked up the phone to dial her parents so that she could set a time up to speak with them when she realized that it was only seven in the morning. She had to wait an hour, so she began going over what little evidence she had on her case, beginning with viewing the video from the pizza store again.

After her second cup of coffee and having finished going over the video once again, she called the parents and set up a 9 am meeting with them at their home. She wanted to go into Amanda's room while she was there to see if she could find anything of importance, so she let her dispatcher know where she was headed, then she got into her patrol car and headed out.

The ride to Amanda's parent's home, who lived just twelve miles past where Amanda's car had broken down, did not take as long as she thought and she found that she had arrived ten minutes early. She got out of the car and took a look around the property before she knocked on the front door, where two tearful parents greeted her and let her in. She was offered a drink, which she politely refused, then Amanda's father asked her what she had found out so far. April said, "Before we discuss that I would like to get some basic information from you about Amanda first if you don't mind." They both nodded, so she asked her age, how long she had been at college, who her friends were, places she often frequented, and if they knew of anyone that she had a problem with or perhaps had made threats against her, or if they had any reason to suspect that she had run away from home. Both of her parents boldly told that Amanda had no reason to ever run away.

She already knew some basic information concerning Amanda since she had run a report on her and had seen her driver's license, but she wanted to hear her parent's responses and observe them as they did. Before they had a chance to ask her anything else, she asked if she could look at her bedroom, and they took her to it. The room was very clean and tidy, and looked like a young woman's room would, a few posters hung on the walls, stuffed animals covered the top of her bed, and some family photos hung on the wall. She saw the high school yearbook and went through it quickly, then she opened the drawers on her dresser and checked through that as well. She finished her inspection by looking at her closet, then she saw her laptop on the chair next to her bed and grabbed it before she left the room.

April asked if she could take it with her, promising to return it as soon as possible, and she received permission. She could tell that her parents were very anxious to hear about what progress she had made so far, so she asked them to sit and said, "I have her car at the lab and they are going over it with a fine tooth comb. We have her purse, which was left on the front passenger seat, as well as her cell phone. Once we look into them we will return them to you along with the laptop."

Her mother had tears flowing down her cheeks as her husband tried to comfort her. He had his arm around her and looked at April, then he said, "Please Detective Sanchez, tell me the truth. What do you know so far?" April thought a moment, then said, "All I can tell you for now Mr. Webb is that I suspect foul play. Once I go over the evidence I have and finish speaking with those who know her I hope to know more. We have deputies looking for her as they patrol the area around where her car broke down. As soon as I find something out I will let you know. For now it is important that you stay home in case you receive a call for ransom for her. If you do, I am to be notified immediately, no matter what you are told. We have people that know how to deal with this that can help get her back alive."

The mother said, "You believe that someone took her? My Amanda?" She burst into tears again and Amanda said, "I suspect foul play for now until I am able to uncover more evidence. Now, does she have any friends that she does not get along with or maybe a past boyfriend that you can tell me about?" They told her that she did not have any enemies, and that her last boyfriend was when she was in the tenth grade. She had only recently started seeing Ray Horton after they met at college. April learned that Amanda was living at home to save money while attending college. So far she did not feel that her parents were involved in her disappearance, but she would run background checks on them both to make sure that they were clean. They kept asking her what she knew so far and asked if she believed that she was still alive. She felt bad for them and tried to assure them the best she could.

April felt that she had what she needed from them for now so she promised to let them know any information as soon as she was able to, then she headed back to the station with the laptop. She listed her parents as persons of interest for now, and not suspects. She hoped that her report would be on her desk when she arrived, and she was going to call her two college female friends as soon as she got back. Maybe they knew about someone that Amanda had a run in with from school that only a friend would know about. So far she still believed that someone had taken her that night, and she hoped that maybe a car passing by may have seen it and call in with some information, but that was a long shot she knew. She was going to call the media after she spoke with her two college friends and ask them to put information on her on the air and ask for help from the public in case someone happened to be driving on that road that night that may have seen her car or another vehicle parked near it. It was a long shot she knew, but she would hope for the best.

Driving back to the station, April's cell rang and she saw the caller ID letting her know that her Sergeant was calling her, so she pressed the answer call button and said, "Hey Sarge, what's up?" Sergeant Millie Franz said, "I have some good news for you. We have the court order for the businesses that you requested, so I dispatched two deputies to head over and collect their video tapes. I also see the report you were waiting for on your desk. I believe that the first thing you are going to want to do though when you get back here is to look at the photograph we found on her cell phone. It shows what looks like a white van that was parked in front of her car."

April felt excited and her voice sounded it when she said, "Did we get a tag from it?!" Sergeant Franz said, "No, it was too far away and the storm did not help. When will you return?" April hit the lights on her light bar, pressed down hard on the accelerator, then said, "Be there in twenty minutes." She felt good that there was a photograph of the vehicle that had stopped. That alone was huge, and hopefully the report would have more evidence for her. Her thoughts turned to Amanda again as she focused on her driving, and she hoped that she was doing OK. She knew that she was going to do everything she could to try and find her, and she was not going to give up on her until she found her.

She grabbed her list and held it tight as she drove back, and glanced over at her laptop wondering if it contained anything useful in it. Maybe her two friends may know something that can help as well she thought.

Chapter 4

Amanda heard the lock turning on the door, and she slid back on the bed as fear surged through her body. She held her pillow tightly against her chest as the door opened and she saw her kidnapper. He stood at the door way holding a tray, then he said, "I brought ya something to eat. It ain't much, but you tell me what you like and when I go to the store I'll get it for ya." He walked over to her nightstand and set the tray down then backed up to the door and said, "Eat. I'll come back to get the tray later. Be thinking about what you need cause I'm headed out to get some stuff." He turned to leave then looked around the room and snapped his fingers as he said, "Oh, yeah, sorry. I reckon I forgot to leave ya some toilet paper, hold on."

He left the door open and she heard his footsteps going down a hallway. It sounded like he was walking on a wooden floor, and she stretched as far as she could to look out of the door. She saw a hallway with a lone picture hanging on the wall, and it looked like it was an old family photo on it. She could not really tell who was in it, but she counted four people before he returned with a roll in his hand. He said, "Here you go." He tossed it at her then closed the door behind him. She did not hear it locking for now and knew that he was going to come back soon.

She looked at the tray and saw a bowl with a spoon in it, and a small box of cereal that looked like the kind you get when you buy a snack pack of cereal. She saw the small cup full of milk on the tray and a paper towel instead of a napkin. She was hungry so she felt it was safe to at least eat the cereal, so she grabbed the small box, opened it, and began to munch on it. Since his appearance disgusted her, she would not use his bowl, spoon, or the milk. She did not trust that any of them were very clean or safe to use.

Ten minutes later he walked into the room smiling at her and said, "So, I got a paper and pencil here, now tell me what you like to eat. I uh, I plan on getting you stuff like clothes and all but I gotta get paid first for that. I have enough to get stuff to eat though." She felt like telling him to leave her alone and fought back tears, but she decided to name a few items in order to appease him and get him out of the room. He made some notes, smiled at her again, then said, "Sit tight and don't try nothing funny. I'll be back after a bit." She heard the door locking this time as he left, then there was silence. Once again she began to cry into her pillow, feeling totally helpless and lonely. Suddenly a thought popped into her head, and she felt elated as she thought about her cell phone. She had hidden it next to the passenger side seat, and she was sure that the police would find it. She hoped that the quick photos she took would reveal who this man was that took her prisoner. She finally felt a ray of hope and actually felt that maybe someone would find her soon.

April ran inside the station as soon as she got back and headed straight to her desk. The report from her crime scene unit was on top of it, as well as three color photographs that had been enlarged. She sat and grabbed the photos, then took her time looking at them. The first one was the one that showed what looked like a white or silver van. It was night out and it had been raining, plus she must have been nervous when she took it because it was a bit blurry like she had moved as she snapped it. No license plate was visible on it, so she grabbed the next photo and looked it over. It was similar to the first photo, but this one had a shadow of a lone figure as it emerged from the driver's side of the vehicle. The dark figure was too far away to see anything clear on it, but it looked like a large male to her. It was the next photo that she picked up that got her excited.

What appeared to be a large male, at least six feet tall, stood in front of her car lookin towards Amanda and waiving at her. That last photo showed the tall male standing about ten feet in front of her car. The picture was not clear, so she was not able to see what the man looked like, but he was wearing dark clothing and a hat pulled down over most of his face. The more she stared at it the more convinced she was that this male was a Caucasian.

She wondered if Amanda had tried to take them without showing the man that she had taken it, and maybe that was why she had pushed her cell phone down in between her passenger seat and center console.

She picked up her report next and started going through it. She saw where the only fingerprints they were able to recover belonged to Amanda, and that there had been DNA samples collected. The report stated that it would take several days for the samples to come back from the lab before they could identify who they belonged to. All fingerprints recovered were Amanda's, including those on her cell phone. The next thing she read was that the reason why the car had stalled was due to a dead battery. That meant that Amanda could not turn the headlights on, but there was enough juice left for the four-way flashers to work, as was reported on Deputy Dearing's report.

She continued reading until she saw the section on the footprints coming from the vehicle that had stopped in front of her car. According to the report, the footprints came from a set of Wolverine boots. There was several pictures of those boots attached that showed the type of boot that contained the same tread, and the crime scene people had also measured the prints coming to her car then returning to the parked vehicle. Unfortunately, one could purchase those boots everywhere around the area. From what they had determined, it seemed that her suspicions had been confirmed. The report stated that the prints made coming to her car were those of a person weighing about two hundred pounds, yet those same prints leaving from her car were deeper and it was estimated that the person making those prints weight approximately three hundred and twenty pounds.

April let out a small shout of excitement, then she grabbed her copy of Amanda's driver's license and looked at the weight listed on it. It was one hundred and nineteen pounds. She knew it. The guy was carrying her back to his vehicle, which also told her that she must have been unconscious. She had not seen anything with the footprints that they veered as he would try to keep a struggling woman from escaping his grip. He must have somehow knocked her out cold, then simply picked her up and walked away with her. Maybe he carried a taser on him. Maybe he had talked her into letting him help her get her car started, then maybe she allowed him to get too close. He must have opened her door then either punched her or maybe even used a stun gun on her.

The report also stated that they believed the person wearing those boots stood about six foot to six foot two inches and weighed about 200 lbs. Next she read that the tire treads belonged to Cooper tires, and it listed what they believed was the size. It was the following information she read that caught her attention. The tire size was the size the large SUV, trucks or full size vans used. She grabbed the photos of the vehicle once again and studied them, then she decided to show them to a few of her deputies. She spoke with four other deputies, her desk sergeant, her dispatcher, and the two ladies that worked in administration, and they all felt that the photograph looked to them to be a van, either white or silver. She also felt that it was a van. A full size white van.

She got an idea and called the local FBI office, then, after identifying herself, she was put through to speak with Special Agent Sharon Foster. She explained her case to her then told her about the photographs, and asked if she could help identify the vehicle and hopefully a license plate number from the photographs. Special Agent Foster said, "We have a FACE Services Unit that uses face recognition technology to identify people. Send me copies and I'll see what they can find for you. They may be able to take a closer look at that vehicle with their technology for you as well. April thanked her and called her lab, then asked them to make more copies and forward them to Special Agent Foster's attention at the FBI office in Hot Springs. Maybe they would be able to make the photographs a little clearer for her and shed some light on the lone figure in the dark and on the vehicle.

She went back to her report and also read that Amanda had

made only one call that evening, and it was to 911. She felt that she probably did not want to frighten her parents, but wondered why she had not called her father or boyfriend to ask for help. So now she had an idea that the person who had stopped was most likely a male weighing approximately two hundred pounds and was approximately six feet tall. The vehicle looked like it was a white van to her, and she began to feel that Amanda had to be unconscious when she was carried back to the van. Amanda Webb, in her opinion, had been kidnapped. She had to meet with the Sheriff next and make him aware of what she knew so far, so she called his office and requested to meet with him in an hour.

First she wanted to speak with the two college friend females whose names Ray Horton, Amanda's boyfriend, had given her. She grabbed her notes and found the two names, then she dialed the first woman on the list, Shawanda Floyd. They spoke for about ten minutes and she learned that she had not seen her in three days. They had kept in touch by texting, and the subject had been about school and their boyfriends. She was also shocked to hear that her friend had disappeared, but confirmed that Amanda was well loved by everyone and that, to the best of her knowledge, had no enemies at all. The second friend April spoke to was Mindy Lewis, and the conversation with her matched that of Shawanda's. Both ladies were stunned and saddened to hear about their friend, and April felt that they both had told her the truth. Both had confirmed to her that they believed Amanda and her boyfriend got along very well and had never had any fights or problems. Still, since she had gathered information on both of them, she was going to do a background check on them as well while she ran one on Amanda's boyfriend and her parents.

She dropped the names off with her Sergeant and asked her to run all of the background checks while she went to meet with Sheriff Lee Thomas. April made the drive to the main Sheriff's Department in Hot Springs and was ushered into his office right away. Sheriff Thomas was a tall and large man, whose tall frame commanded respect from those he met. He had a reputation of running a tight department, and although he demanded a lot from his deputies, he was a fair and honest individual well admired and respected by his employees and by the community.

April gave him a complete breakdown of her case, then he asked her some questions, and said, "I tend to agree with your assessment of this case. I do think that this young lady was indeed kidnapped. I also am glad that you turned to the Bureau to ask for their help and think it is best if we bring them in on the case as well to consult with us. I want you to take lead on the investigation, but work with the FBI and draw from their resources. Anything that we can use at our disposal to help get this young lady back safely and soon is the utmost priority." April nodded her agreement, then he leaned back and smiled at her.

Sheriff Thomas said, "I actually had just signed off on your promotion yesterday April, and was working on a promotion ceremony in front of your peers to make it official. However, due to the fact that you are already doing the job of a detective, I see no reason to delay the promotion for some ceremony. Congratulations, you are now a detective with the Garland County Sheriff Department. Your pay will be made retroactive to the first day you began the investigation. You are not to take on any more patrols effective immediately, and I will make sure your supervisors are aware of it. For now you can stay at the sub-station until you finish the case, but afterwards you will transfer here to my location and work out of this office." April felt glad that her hard work was finally paying off, and she thanked Sheriff Thomas before heading back to her office.

He told her that he would contact the FBI and have them coordinate a meeting with her, then offered his support to her if she needed any help on the case. She felt good inside as she made the drive back, and her thoughts once again turned to Amanda. She had no idea where she was at, or even if she was still alive, but she was going to stay focused on finding her no matter what.

Chapter 5

At the local Walmart, he went through every isle in the food department looking for as much food and snacks he could buy with the ninety four dollars he had to spend. At the time he had seen his young prize stranded on the side of the road, he had not thought about the fact that he now had to feed another mouth, and was now feeling the effects of it. It would be easier if he could get ahold of more money. Maybe if he had more money he could spend more time with her and not worry about doing so much fishing in order to survive.

As he stood waiting in the check-out line, he began thinking about his woman. He had not done anything to hurt the young woman, but if she gave him a hard time he would have to teach her a lesson. He knew that he had to break her and let her know that she was his property now, but he believed that she would do his bidding or suffer the consequences. He looked around at other people in the store and smiled to himself thinking that none of them had a clue about what he was doing. He had felt pride when he had walked the isles because he knew that he had the perfect situation. He had a beautiful young woman that would do his bidding now, and he did not have to coddle her in any way. He owned her and he could do whatever he wanted to with her. He really enjoyed the power he felt he had, and seriously thought that he had to be the luckiest man in the state.

He knew that the one thing hurting him was lack of money. He got paid two times a month, and the amount depended on his haul of fish. Once he got back home he was going to have to go and check his trot lines, then set them up with bait once again. His life was not easy, he was the only one that had the responsibility to earn his income. If he felt sick, he still had to go out for the fish. If it was cold or raining, he still had to go out to fish. If he did not produce, he did not eat. What he needed real bad was to come into some serious cash. Maybe a robbery was what he needed.

He started thinking about where he could go to grab some money without getting caught, then as he approached the checkout register his answer came to him as he watched an old lady in front of him reach into her purse and pull out an envelope full of cash to pay for her items. That was it. He had to rob old people. They always had money. Some more than others. He had to rob the right kind of old people . The old, rich ones, the ones that would be easy targets. He paid for his items and hurried out to the parking lot to look for the old woman, but she was already gone, so he began to look around the parking lot. He knew that there were security cameras there, so he would not risk doing something stupid there, but a thought occurred to him then and now he knew the perfect place to go where he would see a lot of old people at, the local library.

He headed back home and checked on his woman, then gave her some snacks and bottled water before he headed out to check his trot lines. Once he gathered his fish and set new baits out, he drove his route and sold the catch to his restaurant customers. Now that his time was free, he made the drive to Hot Springs Village and headed straight to the local library. Here was a treasure of old people, and it would be here where he would find the perfect target to go after. He began by looking at the cars that pulled in, then, when he spotted a Cadillac, he waited for the owner to come out.

The old woman did not disappoint and showed up less than twenty minutes later. He saw that she was nicely dressed and figured that she had to have money, so he began to follow her to her home, keeping back far enough where she would not suspect him. Once she pulled into her driveway he noted the mailbox number and kept driving by slowly. He drove around the neighborhood to familiarize himself with the streets, then he picked out an escape route in case he would need one. He drove back to the home and parked the van one house before it and across the street from it, then he began to look closely at her property.

The house was a stand-alone home with a large front yard containing a lot of large trees and shrubbery. It appeared like a nice home in an upper class neighborhood, so he figured that people here did not worry much about money. He did not see any other vehicles or people around her home, and he did not see any signs of a large dog either. He could not see any security cameras in the front of the house, and this brought a thin smile to his face. He would return there at night and break in, then he would leave with a wad of cash.

He knew that he had to wear a ski mask so that she would not identify him, and that he would have to tie her up so that he had time to get away. He began thinking about small details like wearing gloves so that he did not leave any fingerprints behind, and parking the van in the back of the house when he came late at night so that the neighbors did not see it, and even driving in with his headlights turned off. He started the engine and pulled away slowly, not taking his eyes off the front of her home. He was coming back later that night to get his cash, and the old woman had no idea that she was about to help him be able to live a better life.

He made it home and checked in on the woman, then thought about what he would call her. He had been so focused on grabbing her and getting out of the area so fast that he had not thought about her purse. He didn't even know who she was. He would ask her name and if he liked it he would use it, if not, he would change it to whatever he wanted. He thought that by now she should be on the news, so maybe he could learn her name and at the same time find out what the cops were up to, so he turned his television on. He had this one on a satellite dish unlike the one he had in her room, so he received excellent coverage.

Not to disappoint, the news channel was showing a story about her so he listened in intently. He learned that she was 20 years old, and that her name was Amanda Webb. He felt a little fear at first as he watched, especially when he saw a news conference given by the Sheriff, Lee Thomas. He feared that man and began wondering if he had made a big mistake by taking her. Then the Sheriff introduced a woman detective named April

Sanchez and told the audience that she was heading the case with help from an FBI Task Force.

He swallowed hard as he learned that the FBI was in on it as well, then he crept up to his window and peered out. Did they already know who had taken Amanda? He looked back and forth at the coverage on the screen, then back outside his front yard area, eventually calmed down as he realized that when he had taken her that night no one had seen a thing. The fact that the cops were asking people for help if anyone knew anything told him that they had no idea who had her. He relaxed a bit now and felt more assured as the time went on. After the news coverage was over he decided that he was totally in the clear and that by robbing the old woman tonight it would draw their attention away from the missing woman's case. He thought that maybe he was smarter than what he was giving himself credit for. Smarter even than the police and the FBI together.

He made some dinner for himself and fed Amanda, then told her to behave and not do anything stupid because he had something to do. He grabbed an old backpack and put some zip ties in it, a roll of duct tape and some rope, then he grabbed his large hunting knife and stuffed it inside next to his 50,000 volt taser. He took the box of rubber gloves, grabbed his keys, then headed out the door. It was time to make some money.

Detective April Sanchez. April was trying to get used to her new title as her co-workers congratulated her back at the sub-station in Hot Springs Village. She received a call that she had to attend a news conference where Sheriff Thomas would ask the public for assistance in identifying Amanda's abductor, introduce the FBI Task Force, and introduce her as the lead detective working the case. Once she had returned to the sub-station she had arranged a meeting with the FBI Task Force members that would take place at her office there since they wanted her to take them to the sight where Amanda had been abducted.

Her co-workers gave her the usual ribbing, then they all congratulated her and told her that they had her back on the case when she needed them. She felt glad that she worked with such great people and began going over every bit of evidence that she had on her case to make sure that she had not missed any important facts. The agent she had spoken with from the task force had offered to review all the store videos as well and told her that they would check in on the photographs she had sent and bring them to the meeting once they were ready. She believed that with them on board now her case stood a better chance of being able to find Amanda.

April's desk phone rang, and she saw that it was an internal call from her crime scene unit. The technician on the line said, "Detective Sanchez, we looked at the laptop you gave us. There is mostly college related materials from her school on it. The emails from her friends and boyfriend, Ray Horton are all innocent. We could not find anything indicating any issues of any kind on it at all. Also, the lab report from the DNA evidence we submitted came back, and unfortunately the DNA does not register with any known criminals, sorry." She thanked him and hung up, then felt a little down after hearing the news.

It was just turning grey outside. That period of time when one knew that darkness would envelope the area very soon. He had made the drive to the old woman's home, drove slowly past it, then made the drive around the neighborhood to make sure that his escape route was clear. By the time he returned to her home it was dark out and he saw that she did not have any outside security lights turned on. Perfect.

Checking his mirrors to make sure that he had no one coming in either direction, he made the turn into her long driveway and drove in slowly with his headlights turned off. His eyes were adjusted, so he had no trouble seeing as he pulled in behind the home. He could see some lights on inside the house but did not see her looking out of the window as he parked the van. Putting the gloves on, he grabbed the knife from the backpack, put the pack on his back, then walked towards the rear of the house. He saw a door in the back of the home and figured that he could get in through it, then surprise the old woman once inside. Once he reached it, he pulled the black ski mask down over his face, placed the blade of his hunting knife on the door lock, then gave it a quick pull. The door popped open easily, and he stepped into what was the kitchen of the home.

Closing the door behind him, he stopped for a moment to listen, and heard the television on in another room. He planned on doing this job as fast as he could then tie the old woman up and leave, so he began to walk down a hallway heading towards the sound of the television. Just as he cleared the hallway and looked into the living room, he felt a sharp pain on the side of his face as he tumbled forward and fell to the ground, dropping his knife on the floor. He yelled out, more in surprise than in pain, as he fell, then looked up from the floor to see the old woman wielding a large walking stick at him. He managed to move just in time as it came crashing down on the floor where he had just been laying.

He jumped up quickly, dodged another strike, then lunged at her. He caught her as she lifted the heavy stick in the air once again and dove into her torso, causing the two of them to fall to the floor. He landed on top of the old woman, then he raised up, struck her with a left hook that twisted her head and forced her to release her grip on the walking stick. He scrambled off her, picked his knife up off the floor, then without realizing it, he struck. He heard the heavy thud as the large blade plunged into her chest, then he heard her gasp and saw her eyes widen like saucers in a look of surprise.

He was breathing heavily now as he looked at the old woman who was lying on the floor with her mouth and eyes open, then he noticed that she was not breathing or moving at all. He closed his eyes once he realized what he had done, then slowly stood up, pulled the blade out of her body, then stood there looking at her not believing what had just happened. He looked at her again and saw that her face had frozen in fear, her eyes and mouth were still wide open. He was stunned as he thought of what had just happened. He bent down and wiped the blood off the blade on her robe, then let out a deep sigh.

Somehow the old lady had heard him entering and had surprised him, clubbing him with that large stick. As his breathing slowly returned to normal he realized what he had just done, so he hurried and began going through the house looking for money. It took him thirty minutes to find where she had kept her cash, finding it, of all places, in an old shoe box inside her bedroom closet. Worried that he had taken too much time there, he took another quick walk around the house to make sure that he had not missed any more cash, then he looked down at her as he walked past the lifeless body and said, "You stupid old woman! None of this would have happened if you weren't stupid."

He made his way to the kitchen, opened the rear door and stepped outside before removing his black ski mask and took in a long, deep breath. That was when he felt the blood on the side of his face. The only light out was from the moon as he ran to the van and climbed inside, then he pulled his visor down, started the engine, and took a look at his face. She had caught him real good and now he had a steady flow of blood running down the side of his face. As he looked at himself in the mirror he saw the gash that she had made with that large stick and he knew that he would have to put some stitches on it. Panicking now as he thought that if he was stopped by the police he was dead meat, he looked around the van until he saw an old rag, grabbed it and held it tight to the side of his face, then pulled out of the back of the house.

He made the turn on the paved road and drove for around fifty yards before he remembered to turn the headlights on, then he accelerated and left the area. Once he made it to Route 298 he remembered to slow down and drive just under the speed limit in order to not attract the attention of any cops around. He cursed as he drove and blamed the old woman for what she had done. All he wanted to do was to rob her, tie her up, then leave, but she had ruined everything. Now he had a murder on his hands. He cursed again, over and over, louder each time, as he drove back home.

Looking down at his backpack, he remembered that he had stuffed all of the cash from that shoe box into his backpack without taking the time to count it. He had no idea how much he had found, but was glad that at least his trip had not been a complete waste. The next time he pulled a job like this he would be ready. He would bring his taser with it in his hand and use it, then he would not have to deal with any issues from his next victim. After locking the gate behind him he felt much better knowing that he had made it home without anyone seeing him. It was time to get cleaned up and clean and stitch his wound, then he would check in on Amanda before turning in for the night. He saw his hands shaking as he walked into the bathroom, then his body shivered as he thought about the old woman's expression as her lifeless body stared up at him.

Once he finished, he had cleaned a three inch cut on the right side of his temple, placed a rag in his mouth as he poured rubbing alcohol on the wound, stitched it up, then covered it with a bandage. The look of shock on Amanda's face when he opened her door and checked on her was enough to let him know that he would have to stay at home for the next few days until he could remove his bandage. He also knew that she had heard him screaming when he cleaned his wound. No sense in alerting anyone that he had that thing on the side of his face and arise any suspicions, so for now he would need to stick around the house until he looked normal again. He locked her door and headed to his room with the backpack, then poured the cash on his bed and began counting it. A big smile came to his face when he finished counting and realized that he now had just over two thousand dollars from that haul. Even though the old lady died, he felt that it had been more than worth it.

The cash brought a smile to his face again as he swallowed some Tylenol before falling asleep. In the morning he would watch the local news to see if the cops had found the old woman's body, then he would need to take his trot lines in. This time he would not set fresh baits on them because he knew that he would not be able to visit his accounts until his face healed and he could remove his bandage. He would need to keep the fish on ice until he could make another delivery in a couple of days. At least he had a lot of cash to enable him to hold out for a long time. Having to supply the needs of another person now, he realized that he would need a steady flow of cash if he wanted to minimize his time on the road. He began thinking about the pros and cons of having the woman there with him. Liking the idea of having her there, he knew that he needed more money. All that he had to do was to rob a few more old people, and there were plenty of them around. He would be ready the next time though, and no one would surprise him again.

He closed his eyes and fell asleep quickly that night as Amanda lay on her bed crying, hoping that there was someone out there looking for her. She had tried to watch the news on the old television in her room and tried to catch some news on the radio, but the reception was terrible and she had not been able to see or hear much at all. She prayed hard and thought about her family as she fell asleep that night. The last thoughts in her head were of the words her captor had spoken to her. He had told her that he expected her to cooperate with him when it came time for him to come into her room and force her to have sex with him.

She shuddered as she thought about it, then more tears flowed from her eyes. She knew then that she would need to come up with some sort of plan to fool him and enable her to make an escape. She believed that he was strong and could easily over power her, but she also believed that she was smarter than he was. Maybe what she needed to do was to fool him, to somehow trick him, then make her escape from this hellish nightmare. What she needed to do was to come up with a plan, then be bold enough to execute it. If not, who knew what was to become of her? Again it was difficult to get some sleep, waking often and gasping as fearful thoughts entered her mind.

Chapter 6

Detective Sanchez, having just returned from the scene where Amanda had been abducted at, now sat across the table from Special Agents Sharon Foster and Brad Lamb in the small conference room at the sub-station sipping on some hot coffee. Now that they both had looked at the scene of Amanda Webb's disappearance, they went over the case first before Agent Foster pulled the photographs her FACE Services Unit had worked on at the request of Detective Sanchez.

The task force members, headed by Special Agent Sharon Foster, had already studied all of the evidence that April had shared with them, when Agent Foster said, "Detective Sanchez, since we are going to be working on this case along with you I want you to know that we are here to assist you. We want to bring Amanda home as bad as you do, so anything that you need from us in the way of assistance is now available to you, and please call me Sharon. I believe that we do not have to be so formal." April smiled at her and said, "Thank you Sharon, and call me April. I appreciate you all being involved in this, and yes, I want to get Amanda home real bad. I just hope that she is still alive."

Sharon stood up and began to pace slowly as she said, "Because the evidence points to an abduction, it is quite possible that she is even though there has not been a ransom request. We need to figure out who took her and why. I know that there has not been a request for ransom, plus she does not come from an affluent family, so it is my belief that she was taken for a few other possible reasons. One is so that the kidnapper took her for sexual reasons, another is for human trafficking. There is one more possibility that I can think of, and I hope that this was not why she was taken, and that is because we have some sick serial killer on our hands that plans to kill her. This is why we must find her as soon as possible. Any one of those reasons means bad news for Amanda. It is, in our opinion, most likely an abduction that was not planned first."

April knew that she was right, and said, "The video evidence did not show any vehicles following her, so I believe that it was an opportunity that presented itself, and her abductor could not resist. The media has her face plastered on the screen and on newspapers right now. If anyone saw anything we should receive some calls soon. I realize that we will receive some crank calls and calls from crazies about it, and that we will have to waste time checking into those leads, but hopefully someone saw something that night and may call in. I need to start by checking criminal records to see if we have anyone living in the area that was previously charged with abduction or rape, and did time for it, and has recently been released. I recall a case from this area years ago where a man was charged locally for kidnapping and raping a young woman. She was freed thankfully."

Sharon said, "Great idea. While you do that Agent Lamb, I mean, Brad, and I will pour through the video recordings again to see if we can find anything. We have Amanda's information out so that people are aware of her abduction, so hopefully it helps bring us some information. I also want to double check her friends and family once again. We can be sure to rule them out and only focus on finding her abductor." With their help, April would be able to focus her attention on finding the kidnapper and not have to spend time interviewing people or double checking video footage, and that made her feel great.

They exchanged phone numbers and agreed to meet there in two days to go over the case again if they had not found Amanda, and the meeting broke up. April went on her laptop and began searching the national criminal data base, focusing on her state, then on her area, to see if any recent criminals with a history of abduction or rape had recently been released from prison. She then began her search for kidnappings in Garland County and ran across the one she had thought of. The name of the kidnapper was George Feller, and he had been arrested five years ago and was sent to prison. She looked up the name of the prison where he was sent to, then called the warden and identified herself.

Warden Bellows asked her to hold as he checked his records, then he came back on the phone and said, "Yes Detective Sanchez, George Fellers was sent here, but unfortunately he passed away three years ago while in custody. Since I began working here only last year, I am personally not familiar with him. The record states that he was killed by a fellow inmate after an altercation. The inmates manage to make weapons from time to time even though we have strict searches. Apparently an inmate had made a knife while working in the prison shop and used it to fatally stab Mr. Feller to death during their fight. The record indicates that the two men fought over food. Senseless isn't it?"

April thanked the warden and crossed Feller's name off her list of suspects., but she noted that he had been caught at his home, and it was not far from her location. She was able to find two more names of recently paroled prisoners living within a twenty five mile radius that had done time for rape, so she added their names to her list. She would speak with both of those men for certain, but continued her search on the data base.

The two FBI agents began their work as well. As Agent Brad Lamb poured through each video, one at a time, Agent Foster contacted Amanda's family and friends and began meeting with them once again to see if anyone of them were involved in her abduction. Knowing that no request for ransom from the kidnapper had been made, it worried her that Amanda was in far greater trouble than anyone realized. She had to help find her as soon as possible.

Early that morning Amanda heard her door being unlocked, then saw her abductor walk into the room carrying a tray of food. She saw the white bandage on the side of his face and wondered what had happened, but he set the tray down, told her to eat, then left the room quickly. She saw the cereal box, breakfast bar, and banana on the tray and grabbed them, then the door opened again and her abductor appeared holding a cup of coffee in his hand. He said, "I have hot coffee, and there is cream and sugar if you want some. I only have a few Styrofoam cups left, so if you want one keep it for the next time til I get some more at the store." She nodded at him, then said, "Thank you, I just drink it black."

He placed the hot coffee on her night stand, and she saw the key ring hanging from his belt before he stepped back. He stood at the doorway looking at her, his eyes boring into her soul. She felt a tinge of fear because she knew that it was only a matter of time before he would enter the room wanting something more than to feed her or give her coffee. She looked up at him and held her gaze, then he said, "I'll come back for the tray in a bit." He closed the door without locking it, then she began to eat her food.

She knew that she had to get ahold of that key ring hanging on his belt. It was the only way she would be able to free herself. He was big and strong, so she knew that she would never be able to overpower him, so she needed to think of a way to get ahold of those keys. Her mind began to work as she munched on her food, and for the first time since being brought here she began to feel a bit of control over her situation because she knew that she had a purpose now. She was going to concentrate on getting herself freed up and getting away from this madman as soon as she could, but she would need a plan first.

He went into the bathroom to look at his wound, and after removing the bandage, he saw that the stitching job he had done did not look good. There was a bit of puss forming from the wound, so he began to clean it with rubbing alcohol. One thing he did not need now was to get an infection. He placed a new bandage on his face then went to his room and took a local map out from his closet. He wanted to see what the area looked like just north of Cortez Golf Club. Hot Springs Village was listed as the most expensive place to live in the state of Arkansas, so he knew that any old people living there are bound to have some money.

The trouble was that both the Sheriff Department and the local Hot Springs Police Department had stations in that area. If he was going to rob one of those residents at the Village he had to make sure that he picked the right location. He would need access in and out of the area quickly, a home that was somewhat secluded, not close to nosy neighbors, and that seniors lived in the home. He figured that once he hit another house and hauled a good amount from it he would have more than enough to be able to take things easy and stay at home.

The next old person he would rob after that had to be from someplace further away though since he wasn't about to risk bringing attention to this area. He knew that he had been real lucky to have run into Amanda broken down on a dark road that wasn't heavily used normally. He was also lucky that there had been a storm that night that had kept most people at home. He wanted to give his face a few more days to heal so that he would not need to wear a bandage, then he would begin to look around the Cortez Gold Club area. He went to the bedroom closet and grabbed his taser and placed a new battery in it, then he checked his supplies of zip ties and duct tape. He was in good shape with supplies, so his next move was to begin to scout around that area.

He studied the map some more as he took it to the living room because he wanted to hear the news. The more he learned about the investigation going on as the cops looked for Amanda, the better off he would be. Although he felt a tinge of fear about having killed the old lady, he wasn't real worried since he knew that no one had seen a thing, plus he had worn rubber gloves and a ski mask.

As Detective Sanchez looked through the arrest records of her two suspects, one of her deputies named Sonya Young came into her small office and said, "Hey April, sorry, I mean Detective Sanchez" April smiled at her and said, "Sonya, please continue to call me April. We're friends here. What's up?" Sonya said, "Well, I heard about the vehicle you believe was a white van you discovered at the scene of that girl's car and I figured that you'd be interested in watching a video I have. I responded to a call about a woman not answering her phone. Her daughter was concerned that she may have fallen and she lives in South Florida, so she called and asked us to check on her mother. When I arrived at the residence I took a look around, then I discovered a rear door on the home which appeared to be broken into. Once I entered I discovered the woman lying on the floor with a puddle of blood around her. She was stabbed to death. I did a quick search and found an old shoe box on the floor of her bedroom and her closet open. All the drawers in the home were open and in disarray from what appeared to be a home invasion and robbery."

April sat forward on her desk and said, "Go on." Sonya nodded then said, "I called the crime scene in when I called dispatch. They sent Detective Saunders from the main branch to investigate, then he had me go door to door to ask if any of the neighbors had seen or heard anything and to check for security cameras. No one saw or heard a thing, and the only security camera in the neighborhood was two doors down and across the street from the woman's home. The home owner played the tape for me and I saw a white van as it passed both ways. I have the tape here and figured you may want to take a look. He told me that he often forgets to turn it on, so hopefully we'll get lucky. The home owner was able to transfer the recording right to my phone."

April pointed to a chair and said, "Thanks Sonya, let's have a look." They both saw the white van as it drove by slowly heading east, then one hour and twenty minutes later, the same van drove by again, only this time it was driving much faster and in the opposite direction. April rewound the video and stopped it as the van passed by the camera the first time. They were able to make out a figure in the driver's seat but the camera lens was too far away to be able to recognize the driver's face. She said, "Sonya, forward this to me please. I'll have the FBI take a look at it and see if they can do something with it, and thanks for being on your toes. This could end up being the same vehicle that was at scene of the abduction, great job!"

April forwarded the recording to Special Agent Foster with a message about the home invasion. Agent Foster texted her that she would forward it to her FACE Services Unit and get back in touch with her. April called Detective Saunders, who worked out of the main Sheriff's Department and asked about the murder. Ben Saunders, a veteran of eighteen years, said, "First of all congratulations on the promotion. Yeah, this woman, Mrs. Dolores Richards, was seventy one years old. Her daughter is on the way here right now from Florida. It seems that someone broke into the home from the rear entry and that they were confronted by her. We found a large, wooden walking stick with traces of blood on it, so I believe that she must have hit the robber hard with it. The robber retaliated and killed her by stabbing her in the chest. My guess is that the blade hit the heart because there was a lot of blood pooled on the floor by the time we arrived. The house was ransacked and a shoe box empty that I bet had something valuables inside like cash or jewelry. I called all the pawn shops in the area and put them on alert in case there was jewelry stolen. It appears to be a robbery gone bad."

April said, "I gather you are aware of the only video around." He said, "I have a copy of it, but was not able to get a plate nor make out the driver. It came on her street driving slowly, then a little more than an hour later sped past the camera as it headed out of the area. It's the only thing I have so far. The crime scene unit swept the home so I'm waiting for the autopsy report and for their report on the DNA from the blood on the walking stick. Maybe we'll get lucky and get DNA or prints that we can match. Why are you interested?"

April told him about the van, then they began to contemplate if the same person was involved. April said, "I had a thought. It may be way off, but I wonder if the same man did this in order to get some money. That area is affluent, and he may have known that. Having to provide for a kidnapped victim means more food to buy." Detective Saunders said, "It's not a crazy thought. Maybe the guy that did this is kind of poor. That van seemed to be old, like a 2010 or so. I used to own one years ago that I used to paint houses on the side when I wanted some extra cash." April thanked him and he told her he would forward copies of his reports to her, then she ran the idea past FBI Special Agent Foster. She also told her that her thought was not a bad one, so April grabbed a cup of coffee and began to think about it some more before she headed out to speak with her two new suspects.

Chapter 7

Amanda heard the door unlocking and sat back on her bed holding the pillow against her. The man stood at the doorway and stared at her, and she could see the bandage on his head. He came up to her bed and looked around, then he said, "Just checking on you. I know that you're scared, but as long as you listen to me and do what I tell you everything will be fine. I want you to know that I do not want to hurt you, but I will punish you if you fight me or resist me. I own you now. This is your home now, understand?" She nodded at him only but did not respond.

He sniffed, then said, "Well, that's all for now. There's some things I gotta do for the next few days so try and relax. I'll be in and out. In a few days I'm going to the store to shop, so give me a list of what clothes you need. You know, women stuff and what size underwear you use, stuff like that. I have a washer machine here and a clothes line out back to dry clothes. When your sheets need washing let me know. I'll get ya some clothes to use while yours are in the wash. I'll get ya some books and magazines too. Like I said, the nicer you treat me the nicer I treat you. Don't get no ideas that you can run away from here. I have three big dogs I keep outside and they will tear you to pieces if you ever managed to get out." She watched him remove the larger key from the key ring on his side as he stepped out and locked her door.

He left the room and started to watch the news. Having lied to her about having dogs was brilliant he thought. That lie just came to him at that moment, but he saw the look of fear on her face when he told her. He sat back and sipped on a cold beer as he watched the reporter describe the scene and tell everyone about the murder of a woman named Dolores Richards. He shivered when he heard the word murder being used by the news anchor, but he watched to hear what the police knew so far. He learned that some Detective named Saunders was investigating what they described as a home invasion. He smiled when the anchor said that the police did not have any suspects, and he did a fist pump at that moment. Easy money, well, almost, he thought as he rubbed the side of his head.

He had not felt bad for having killed the old lady. Afterall, she hit him first. What if she had killed him? He had a right to defend himself he thought. Regardless, he had made a good haul from that place and he knew that there was more cash to be had in the Village. He grabbed the map again and studied the area around the golf course as he sipped his beer. In another day or two at most he would be ready to go and grab more cash. Today he wanted to take a look at several places that he thought might also be good to grab some cash from old people at.

The town of Pencil Bluff was just about an hour away from where he lived, maybe less. He knew that there was an RV park there because he and his brother had delivered a load of fish there years ago for some huge celebration they had. They had paid them well in cash and had even given them a bonus for delivering the fish so quick. He remembered that the park was large and that the residents there had a lot of room between the homes there, plus the area was secluded and he had seen new, expensive looking motor homes parked there. A place like that would be easy to get in and out at night and get away without anyone seeing him. He also thought about the town of Washita which was only about a half hour away. He had been there a long time ago with his brother after hearing about a community dance. They both saw some nice looking houses there, so those people must have some money. He should have been doing this all along and not have wasted his life fishing for some stupid fish and scraping a meager living. He had now decided where to go, so he figured that since Wachita was on the way to Pencil Bluff, why not check both places out. He was pleased that he was being real smart with his planning, and he felt that soon he would holding a ton of cash in his hands. Free cash.

He loaded some food into the van, checked in on Amanda, then took off. He was wearing a cowboy hat over his head that covered most of the bandage, and he was not getting out of the vehicle anyway so he felt that it was safe to go. With the extra cash he now had he felt hopeful that he could get even more and be able to live the type of life that he always wanted and deserved. Unlike his brother who had not taken precaution and had paid a price for his actions, he was too smart to repeat those mistakes. He was going to be able to enjoy the fruits of his labor soon, and wondered again why he had waited for so long to come up with the idea of getting himself some easy money and enjoy life's pleasures.

The drive to Washita took about thirty minutes, and he had to slow down for fear of driving through it. This wasn't what he had remembered from before. At that time, there were all kinds of people milling about the main street having a good time, and there was no room to park. Booths were set up where vendors sold food and he remembered the music. It was loud and it played everywhere. Now the small town was quiet, and he only saw a stray cat on the side of the road. It felt frustrating to see that the houses did not seem belong to rich people like he had thought, so he pressed the accelerator and continued on to the town of Pencil Bluff. He knew that the RV Resort was there for sure, and he was determined to find out where some new RV was parked at that belonged to rich, old people.

Another thirty minutes of driving and he entered the out-skirts of the town. He decided to drive through it and get famil-iar with the place. He would need to learn the streets so that he could work out an escape route anyway, and this way he would at least have an idea of what the place looked like. Like most small towns in the country, the usual small shops adorned the main street. Laundry mats, small restaurants, a hardware and several other mom and pop stores were spread out on both sides of the road. He had seen the sign for the RV resort so he now turned around and headed straight for it.

The entrance was wide enough for the large motor homes to come in and out, and he saw the small trailer where the office was located. Driving in like he belonged here, he drove on every street of the small community looking at all of the mobile homes and RV's that were parked there. Some people lived there year around while others rented a space for a short stay. He wished that the community had some sort of outing now so that he could see all of the residents out and about, but he remembered that there was a swimming pool and recreation hall where he and his brother had made a delivery to, so he went there to take a look around.

Parking the van in front of the pool, he saw a small group of people leaving it with towels around their shoulders and laughing with one another. One of those people was a woman that seemed to be in her early sixties. This caught his interest.

After a few minutes the group got smaller as people dropped off once they reached their individual houses, then he saw that there were now only two women left, and one was the woman he was watching, the other slightly younger. The two women walked together until they reached a large RV, then both went inside. He took a good look at the fancy motor home and was pleased, then he drove past it and headed back home. That was where he would return soon to collect his prize. The two women had to be loaded to afford that rig. The next thing he had to do was to get ahold of more money. It was time to make a plan to visit Hot Springs Village once again, then he would return here and pay a visit to the RV. If he managed to get a good haul of cash from those two places he could lay low for a long time and enjoy himself. Maybe give up fishing all together as well.

April learned that the videos Agent Lamb had gone through did not have anything on them that proved helpful. Only one of the videos had recorded Amanda's car passing by on the street that evening, but only a few other vehicles passed afterwards and none were close to her car or were a van. After seeing the video evidence, there were no suspects to investigate from them. Likewise, Special Agent Foster called her and told her that she had interviewed Amanda's parents, her close friends, and the boyfriend, and had not considered any of them to be involved in any way. They were all in the clear, and, according to those same people, Amanda did not have any enemies or anyone that had been upset with her in any way.

This told April and Special Agent Foster that whoever had taken her was a complete stranger. As April thought more about the night Amanda went missing, she believed that she had just become a victim because her car had broken down in the wrong place at the wrong time. Someone passing by saw her then made the instant decision to take her because the situation was too tempting to them to pass up. Because she knew that it was a van stopping there that night she thought about that vehicle as the most likely way to find the kidnapper.

She decided to check on every single business that operated between Hot Springs Village to the small towns of Fannie, Story, and Washita. She also knew that Irons Fork Recreational Area was off Route 298. It drew a lot of people that went there to fish, swim or boat, and the rangers there might have seen the van before. Maybe one of the businesses that operated out of one of those places owned a van, and hopefully it would be a white or silver van that was around eight to ten years old.

April then picked up the phone and called the DMV at Hot Springs, then requested a list of vans owned in the county that had been registered by private individuals or businesses, requesting the list to show vehicles five years old and older. The clerk told her that it would take some time to print it out, so April told her that she would send a deputy there to pick it up once they called her to let her know it was ready. She decided to update her white board with the current information she had on the case so that when she met with anyone in the conference room she could refer to it and point or refer to the most important elements of evidence. Once she finished this, her thoughts turned to the woman that had been killed in her own home and robbed.

The neighbor's video had recorded a van driving by slowly, then returning at a much higher rate of speed as if it was in a hurry to leave the area. If the FBI is able to make anything out of the video that shows it to be the same van as the one that stopped for Amanda, she believed that it was the same person committing both crimes. This would mean for certain that this person needed money and decided that some old lady was an easy target. This also meant to her that it was possible he may strike again. She knew that the most affluent place in the state was Hot Springs Village, and there was both a police presence there as well as her own deputies that patrolled that area.

She sent out a BOLO (Be on the lookout for) to the law enforcement community that worked that area in case this van decided to appear there once again. She felt that once she got the DMV report and started going through the registered vehicles, she may be able to find the van and its owner. Her hopes climbed as she thought about having the task force helping her, and she knew that detective work meant eliminating a lot of possibilities one at a time until the correct one appeared. It would take some time to find this van, but if it was registered in her county she would find it. For now she knew that her patrols were looking for a light colored van, so if this person used any of the local stores around they may run into it. She sent a note to Sheriff Thomas to update him on her and the task force's progress before leaving for the day. She said a prayer for Amanda Webb and asked God to keep her alive and safe.

Chapter 8

Amanda had a tough time sleeping last night as she thought about the kidnapper coming into her room to rape her. She knew that the time was coming soon, and she had cried until her tears had dried up. She knew nothing about him at all, and it frightened her even more. Was he a serial killer, a rapist or a murderer? Had he been in prison before? That morning he came in carrying the tray of food once again, and this time the bandage on his face was smaller. He seemed happy for some reason, and this worried her. She decided to see if she could learn anything about him, so before he left the room she said, "Can I ask you your name? I don't know what to call you." There was silence as he stopped at the door.

Without turning to face her, he spoke with a gruff voice to her and said, "Just call me master. Afterall, I do own you." It seemed that her speaking to him had caught him off guard, so she decided to press on and said, "Can I ask why you brought me here and if you plan on keeping me here for a long time?" Now he turned to face her and she saw his fists balling up. He let out a deep breath, then he raised his tone as he said, "I brought you here cause you now belong to me, and as far as how long, it's however long I decide. Anything else?"

Amanda could sense that he was not comfortable speaking about this and she did not want to anger him so that he would do something she would regret, so she said, "I would like to know more about you, you know, since I'm going to living here from now on. Can you tell me just a little, please? It would be nice to get to know you at least a little bit." She had softened her tone in order to make her voice sound innocent, almost sweet, faked a weak smile, and it worked. He seemed to relax, then he came over to her bed and sat on the corner, and she did her best not to jump back out of fear. She faked a smile at him again, then he said, "Well, OK, but just a little bit. After a while you'll get to know me better, and you'll get to like me. I'm not a bad person.

I just thought that you're real pretty and all and I want you for myself. If I didn't bring you here you would not come here on your own." He stroked her hair as he spoke, and she feared that he was about to make a move on her, but she forced herself to remain still.

She did not respond, giving him time to continue talking. He lowered his tone now and said, "I um, I run my own business. Have for years now. I am very successful and make a good living at it too. Hold on." He stood suddenly and left the room, leaving her door wide open. She stood and walked to the edge as she held her chains so that they did not rattle, and she was able to see the hallway as it emptied into a living room. It looked like an old farm house, and the dark, dirty furnishings matched the look of the owner as well. She hurried back to the bed and sat on it just before he walked in smiling and carrying a wad of cash in both hands.

He showed it to her and said, "See, so that you don't think that I was lying to ya. I make a lot of money. I get paid two times a month, so I will be able to provide for you real easy, especially since I'm about to get a big raise." He smiled at her now and she saw the yellowed teeth, almost gagging her as she quickly glanced down and said, "Wow! That's really good master. What do you do for a living?" He looked around as he thought, then he said, "I own my own business. I run a business that involves fishing. That's all you need to know about it. I work hard and I'm the boss."

She pretended to be impressed, so she smiled at him and said, "That sounds really fine master. What do you like to do when you're not working?" He looked down again then said, "Uh, well, I watch TV. I work real hard and don't have much time for much else I guess. I like to hunt some times. I'm a real good shot too. Maybe I'll get us some rabbit or maybe even a deer to eat. Would you like that?" Not wanting to see an animal die so that this idiot could feel more manly, she said, "Oh, thank you but I prefer not to eat meat. The fish you give me is just fine. Is that some that you catch yourself?"

He smiled at her and said, "Yup, it's all from my trot lines. Like them huh?" She smiled and nodded, then he said, "Later on I gotta head to the store, so have that list ready of what size clothes you wear. I'll bring ya something to read to. Is there anything in particular that you want? If there is, put it on the list and I'll see about getting it for you."

She did not want to have him feel that he was treating so nice that he would demand a payback, so she said, "No, something to read would be nice. I would like a better antenna for the TV here. It's hard to see any channels in here." She smiled again, and he nodded as he walked out, then he said, "Fine, I'll look into that for ya." The door locked once again, and now she knew that he fished for a living. She had noticed that the van had smelled like fish, as well as his own body, so she had already figured that he set out trot lines to catch fish then sold them to make a living.

As far as that wad of cash he showed her, he had it after he got that wound on the side of his head, so she thought that maybe he had robbed someone for it and had received a beating as a result. He was not some successful businessman like he wanted her to believe in order to impress her. His van was old and dirty, as were his clothes, and from what she had seen of the house, it appeared that it was a run down old farm house. She was convinced that he must have robbed someone for that cash. Now she feared for herself even more as she thought that someone capable of doing that and of kidnapping was not a stable human being. Maybe he wasn't a human being at all, but a sick monster pretending to be human.

After she ate he came for the tray and her list, then he said, "Soon me and you are gonna get to know one another real good. You'll see then that I'm not a bad guy at all. I'll be heading out to the store now so behave and don't try nothing stupid. I don't want to punish you, so don't make me do it. I won't be responsible for my temper if you do, and remember that there's mean dogs out there." The door locked, but she had seen the ring of keys on his side again. It seemed that he always kept it on him.

She had to figure out a way to get her hands on it, and a way to buy some time so that she could unlock the chains and run out of the door. She also had to deal with the fact that he owned guns and had some bad dogs outside. It seemed like a lot to overcome, but what choice did she have?

The DMV had left her a message after she had left for home last evening that they had her report ready. April asked one of the deputies to stop by and pick it up on his way back to the station, then she headed to the break room to fill her coffee cup up. She was hopeful that the DMV record would prove useful.

He was ready to go to the store. He wished he made more money so that he did not have cash flow issues. He only had his food and gasoline to pay for, so he had managed to make a living from providing fish to the local restaurants. The old farm house had been paid for, as had the van, and having solar power at the farm enabled him to live without paying for utilities. Sometimes he made out well, other times he scraped by, but he had managed to do OK for himself so far.

After locking the gate behind him, he headed to the local Walmart with his list, and he felt like he was a married man in a way. He liked it better that he was actually an owner instead of a husband, since that was going to provide a much better result for him without the headaches of being involved in a marriage. A sudden sense of fear over powered him as entered the store, and feeling afraid that he may be caught at any moment, he rushed through the isles as he picked up the items on the list, then bought more food, and hurried home before some cop spotted him.

He wondered why he felt fear at times since he knew that no one had seen him take that girl. Maybe he was just being cautious he told himself. Just act normal and everything will be fine he told himself. He began thinking about his woman as he drove back home, and he felt himself becoming excited. A few moments later he felt fear again and continued looking at his rearview and side mirrors as he drove back home.

Chapter 9

The deputy had returned quickly from the DMV with her report, and April went through it quickly, thinking that it was less time consuming than she thought it would be. It listed a total of eight vans in the age group she had requested. After narrowing her list to six vehicles that operated withing a 25 mile radius of an area close enough where she felt someone owning that van would most likely live or work near the site of Amanda's kidnapping, she made her list of the owner's names and addresses, then she called FBI Special Agent Sharon Foster.

Sharon agreed to go along with her since April was also paying a visit to the ex-cons recently released from prison that she had on her list. They met early for breakfast then put the list of van owners together so that they went to see the farthest away owner first, then work their way back as they added the two felons that they would visit first.

The first van was in the town of Washita, and it belonged to a woman named Florence Carter. Although they did not believe that a woman was the kidnapper, they felt they had to check it out anyway in case someone else lived there that they were not aware of. After arriving at the Carter residence and identifying themselves, the old woman laughed when they told her that they wanted to see her van. She said, "Follow me out back." There, up on four blocks, was the old van, and it had been completely gutted on the inside. The old woman said, "Yeah, it's still registered believe or not, but my son is making some kind of art thing with this. He's an artist you know. The stuff inside went to the junk yard along with the motor about four months ago. I guess I'll be needing to return the plate back to the DMV and not have to pay for it no more." She was still laughing when they left the residence, and April and Sharon both started to laugh themselves.

The next van turned out to belong to a church. The pastor showed them the van, then explained that it was not running.

He had asked for donations to see about getting it back on the road again because they used it to pick up the local kids for Sunday school. Both April and Sharon tried to start it before they left.

Knowing that they had to check the two ex-cons next, they headed to see the first one, a man named Vincent Core. Vincent had been released from prison after having served ten years for raping a 67 year old woman after he broke into her home, then beat and robbed her before he raped her. The frown on his face told them that he was not happy to see them at his home. He let them inside and stood by as April watched him while Sharon searched the double wide trailer where he was living. He smiled at them once they began asking his whereabouts and demanded to see the vehicle he owned, then he said, "I just got back last night from seeing my brother over in Tennessee. I'll give ya his name, address, and phone number and you can check. My car is out back."

They checked the old car and asked what king of vehicle his brother owned before calling the number he had given them. Agent Foster called from their car while April kept Vincent on the front of the home by the door, and the story checked out. His brother had confirmed that Vincent had been staying there for the past thirty days. He had come to visit to ask for help in getting a job with him since he owned his own landscaping business, and he had sent him back home to pack with instructions to move in with him and begin working with him. They had no choice but to rule him out once he provided gas receipts from his trip to and from visiting his brother.

The next visit was going to be with the other con recently re leased, so they put his address on the GPS and headed his way.

He was watching the local news again shortly after getting home from the store, then he thought about the fact that the police were still trying to find out who had taken Amanda, and he became angry once again as he watched the news show how there were now increased patrols everywhere. He figured it was best if he would just relax and stay at home for a few days since his nerves were on edge anyway. Maybe he should forget about going back to Hot Springs Village since there were cops all over that place and just go to the RV Resort. No way were the cops suspecting that anything would happen way over there he thought. That thought seemed right to him just then, and he began to calm down, so he got the map out and went over the area in Pencil Bluff once again. He had to get his plans right so that no one would see him or his van. There was no sense taking any chances for now, instead he was going to stay at home for a few days and let things calm down.

The next stop for the two officers was to visit the ex-con named Riley Adams. He had been released three months ago after serving nine years for rape and assault. He had beaten a man outside of a bar one night then, after fighting the man's girlfriend as she tried to defend her boyfriend, he beat and raped her in the back of his truck. He had turned himself in to the law the next day and was given a twelve year sentence, but he got out early on good behavior. The home they pulled into was about a mile from the small town of Story, and was off Route 298. It was a typical small ranch that looked like it had seen better days. The lawn was overgrown with tall weeds and there were several old washing machines, two old rusted cars, and a variety of junk strewn about the front of the home.

As they pulled up to the house a man slid out from under an old Jeep and wiped his greasy hands as he waited for them to approach. Before they had a chance to speak to him he said, "If you're here about the missing young woman I want you to know that I had nothing to do with it." Agent Foster said, "Can you prove it?" He said, "I will take a lie detector test, you can check my prints and take a DNA sample, but I am telling you that I have not done anything wrong. I learned my lesson and do not want to go back to prison. I run my own business now fixing cars and finally started making some decent money. Please, go inside and have a look all you want. I also have someone that can vouch for me, my pastor."

The two women looked at each other, then April went into the house. She did not see anything out of place and was surprised to see that it was clean and well maintained. Agent Foster got the pastor's name so that she could contact him, then she asked Riley to account for the past week. He could only prove his whereabouts during the daytime since he had customers arrive to bring or pick up their vehicles, so they arranged for him to be tested for prints and DNA early the next morning. The pastor vouched for him and felt that he believed that Mr. Adams was sincere about his making a new start. He had been active in the church since his release, and he was willing to vouch for his character.

Satisfied that for now Adams was in the clear, especially since he had volunteered to be tested, they left and headed to the next location on their list of someone that owned an older van. It was on the way back to the station anyway, and it was the first of two more stops they had to make, but so far they had not been able to find the owner of the van, or the vehicle itself.

After memorizing the route on his map to take as an escape route if needed, he finished watching the reporter mention that the investigation was intensifying as he showed Amanda's picture on the screen. Now he worried that the cops had learned something else, and this made him nervous again. He wasn't sure what to make of the story as he paced around the living room. He decided to keep his backpack loaded with all of the cash, the taser and gun, and his supplies, then he set it by the door and looked out of the front window again.

He watched nervously for the next hour, then finally began to believe that he had been worried over nothing. If the cops knew about him they would have come out there already. He started to relax some, then he began to think about Amanda. Maybe it was time for him to get his mind off his troubles and spend some time enjoying her. He licked his lips as he thought about it, but for now he had to focus his attention to getting more money.

Once he had the actual cash in hand he would be able to stay at home and really enjoy his time with her.

The two law enforcement officers had arrived at the dirt road that led back to the Feller residence when April said, "I need to think a second." She stopped the car, then opened her notebook and began going through her notes as Agent Foster watched. April saw her looking at her, then she said, "Sorry, it's just that I just thought of something I read in a report once we turned off Route 298. Remember me telling you that a few years ago a man was arrested for kidnapping that lived around here?" Sharon nodded, then April said, "Well, it just dawned on me that the owner of the van we are about to go and speak with has the same address as the man named Feller that had been arrested."

Agent Foster said, "I thought you told me that Feller had died in prison." April said, "That's what I learned. He was killed inside while serving his time, and the prison warden confirmed it, but now here we are at the same address, and the dirt road was what struck my nerve. I remember reading the report and hearing how the house they raided was like, out in the middle of nowhere. They had a hard time finding it at first since they hadn't even seen a mailbox. Still, the report said that this place was really secluded. It seems that maybe someone else lives here and owns that van according to the DMV report, but that does not make sense."

Sharon looked at her and said, "You mean someone else like possibly another family member?" April nodded, then said, "The report did not mention anything about anyone else being involved, nor did it list a next of kin. Should we call for back up before we head in?" Sharon thought a moment, then said, "Not yet. Let's at least have a look first." They headed up the dirt road slowly as they looked for a side road that would lead to the home, then about a mile later they saw it. There was an old gate that looked like it had not been maintained, plus it was open, so they drove through it, made one turn, then saw an old house up ahead and stopped. Everything there was overgrown with tall weeds and shrubs, and an old rusted piece of what once was a car was in front of the house.

April pulled out a pair of binoculars and began looking closely at the home. A moment later she said, "I don't see a vehicle there, plus the place looks abandoned from here." Sharon took a look next, then she said, "I agree, let's head on up and take a look." They drove up and parked in front of the home, then spread out and cautiously headed to the house with their weapons drawn. The grass was too tall, and it was full of weeds, and two of the windows had been busted out, and they both felt that this place was abandoned. They got up on the front porch, then peered through the window and saw that the place was empty, except for what looked like some garbage that had been left there years ago.

April said, "I don't understand this. The DMV report said that a van is registered to this address, so that means that the address should be a current one." Sharon said, "We didn't see a mailbox out front. We need to look into this closer because it doesn't make sense to me either. Let's finish with the rest of our list, then we can head in and check this out."

Amanda heard the door being unlocked and scooted back on her bed as her kidnapper walked in carrying some items. He said, "I got ya some clothes and underwear here, plus a few magazines and a picture book for ya to look through. I also got more food for us." He was smiling at her and it creeped her out. She watched him set the items down on the small table, then he turned and said, "The time is coming when me and you will get together. Remember what I done told ya, you treat me nice and I treat you nice." He left the room and she began to shiver.

Chapter 10

The rest of their day had not produced any results from the DMV report and April was upset about it. She had felt certain that they would have been able to match one of the names on the report with the owner of the van that she was looking for. They headed back to the sub-station feeling frustrated, then they went through the report once again as Sharon went to grab two coffees.

They spent the next two hours going through the report after having expanded the search radius from the spot of the kidnapping from a 25 mile one to a 40 mile one. They only ended up with one other vehicle that they felt they had to check out, and it was about 30 miles away. Sharon said, "It's possible that the van owner was on his way home when he spotted Amanda and could not let such an opportunity pass by. Maybe the kidnapper lives far away. It feels like we're missing something, but I can't put my finger on it." April said, "I agree. Something is missing here, and I can't figure it out either."

Amanda knew that she was going to be raped soon. Her worst nightmare was going to come true if she did not think of a way out of this mess. She had to get her hands on that key ring, so she began thinking of ways to free herself as she looked around the prison room she had been placed in. He was coming to bring her something to drink soon, and she needed to be ready to make her escape. She felt both angry and nervous as the footsteps on the wooden floor approached.

He walked into her room carrying a large porcelain cup of hot coffee, and she saw her chance of freedom at that moment. She took a quick look and saw the key chain hanging on the side of his belt, then she stood and extended her arms to grab the steaming hot cup from him. He grinned as he handed it to her, then screamed loudly as Amanda hurled the hot liquid at his eyes. She brought her right knee up as fast and hard as she could and caught him in the groin. He went to the ground on both of his knees hard and she raised the cup then sent it crashing on his head as she reached for the key ring. One tug and she had it in her hand, then she kicked out with her leg and caught him under the chin, which bolted him backwards, landing on the floor with both arms spread out. She had seen him reach for the larger key each time he had left the room, so she figured that the smaller one was for the lock on her chains. She placed the key in one of the locks and it popped open instantly, bringing a smile to her face, then she bent and unlocked the chain from her ankle as he started getting up. She heard him growl and begin to cuss as she bolted out of the door, then she placed the large key in the lock and turned it. He was locked inside now.

She was breathing hard now and could feel her heart pounding with fear as she heard him banging on the door from inside the room. She turned and ran to the living room, did a quick search for the guns he said he had, but she did not see any. Amanda saw the front door and just as she was about to open it she remembered what he had said about the dogs. She paused as she heard him pounding and kicking the door as he cursed loudly at her, then she saw the backpack on the floor. The second she picked it up it felt heavy, so she opened it and looked at the contents inside.

A thin ray of hope flashed in her mind as she saw a taser and a pistol, so she grabbed the backpack, threw it over her. And held the pistol out in front of her as she opened the front door. Still feeling the adrenaline of being terrified out of her mind, she stepped out onto the front porch and looked for the dogs. She looked left, then right, but she could not see them. She thought that they could be around back or anywhere on the property. She saw the old van sitting there and wished that she had seen the keys for it, but as terrified as she was now she decided to start running down the dirt road.

Amanda kept looking around as she ran to see if she could spot the dogs, then she turned to see the house again to make sure that he had not gotten out of the room yet. For that brief second she caught her breath before she took one last look around for those dogs. Still seeing no sign of them, she turned and began to run as fast as she could. She had no idea where she was, but she knew that she was on a dirt road that had to lead to somewhere.

He was angry. He felt like his groin was going to explode, and it had taken him a few minutes for his head to clear once he had been kicked hard under his chin. He felt some loose bottom teeth as blood came out of his mouth, then he stood up and let out a loud growl as he began pounding on the door. He cursed at Amanda as his fists pounded constantly on the door. He tried the handle but it was locked, then he cursed louder and began kicking at the door.

Since it was an old wooden door, it was heavy and well built, as was the lock on the door. He had made sure that it had a strong lock on it so that she could not get out, and now he was paying the price for it. He kicked at the lock over and over until his legs felt like rubber, but the last kick finally popped the lock. He used his heavy frame and put his shoulders on the door as he ran into it hard, then it popped wide open.

He let out another loud growl as he headed straight for the living room, then his eyes widened with fear when he saw that his backpack was no longer by the front door that was now open wide. He let out a loud curse again as he looked outside and saw no sign of Amanda, but he saw the van was still there. He turned and ran into his room and grabbed the van keys, then headed back to the room where he had kept Amanda and put his shoes on, then he ran outside and got the van started. Peeling his tires on the dirt road, he made a sharp turn and floored the accelerator. He had to find her or it was going to be real trouble for him. Once he caught her she was going to regret what she did to him because he was going to make her suffer.

Amanda was winded and had to slow her pace. She began to walk and felt weak from lack of proper nutrition, but she knew that if she stopped he would catch her. She finally began to walk at a faster pace, looking over her shoulders from time to time hoping not to see that white van. She had no idea where she was at or where she was going, but at least she was free and now had a chance to get away. The dirt road was covered by thick shrubs and scrub oak trees on both sides, and it seemed to go on forever as she looked ahead. It was quiet and desolate there, and she wondered if she would ever see a paved road as she kept her fast pace up. She felt true fear as she ran, and it was what was keeping her from stopping to take a break.

Thoughts of seeing her family again motivated her to keep going even though she felt tired and scared. She kept looking back, then she ran a little and walked again as she tired. Breathing harder now, sweat ran down her face as the hot sun beat down on her. She was tired and thirsty, but she knew that she could not stop. Without realizing it, she was moaning with fear as she set a fast pace down the dirt road.

Really worried now, he sped down the dirt road, and just after he made the bend on the road he spotted her. He let out a shout as he saw that she was walking down the middle of the road. He smiled as he floored the accelerator, closing the distance between them.

Amanda heard the engine, then turned, saw the white van, and let out a scream as she took off running once again. She looked at the thick shrubs and trees on both sides of the road, then looked behind her once again and knew that she was not going to be able to run down the road anymore. She turned and began making her way slowly through the thicket as the van finally came to a stop right behind her.

She moaned with fear as she burst through the heavy brush, and now she heard him yelling and cussing at her. The noise behind her scared her. It sounded like a bull crashing through the forest, and she knew that he was too close. She managed to get through the worst part of the shrubs, then began to run once again as he cleared the tree line. He let out another growl and took off as fast as he could. Given her weakened state and exhaustion, she was not able to put more distance between herself and the animal chasing her, then she felt her body fly through the air as he threw his large frame at her.

Amanda landed on the dirt, scraping her face on the ground as she slid forward, then his full weight landed on top of her back and she let out a scream as total fear enveloped her. He grabbed her hair and yanked her face up off the ground, then he swung a right hook that caught her on the side of her face. She almost passed out from the heavy blow and now felt dizzy as he turned her body over and cradled her.

Breathing heavily, he sat on top of her and back handed her hard on her face. She felt like vomiting now as she began to see small, white, fuzzy dots through her eyes. Feeling like she was dazed, she struggled to remain conscious as she felt her body being lifted into the air. She heard him yelling and cursing at her, but she could not make out his words as he threw her over his shoulder and began walking back to his van. Her body bounced as she was bent over his shoulders, and all that she could think of was her family. Her body lacked enough liquids in it to allow her to shed any tears, but she wailed out loud as she realized that she had failed.

He opened the rear cargo door of the van then threw her body inside after he took his backpack off her shoulders. He wiped his mouth as he breathed hard, then he zip tied her wrists and ankles then slammed the door shut and began the drive back to his home. He had let his guard down and had paid a price for it, but he would not repeat this mistake ever again. He knew that he had to calm down before he dealt with her or he may end up killing her. He wanted her alive so that he could enjoy using her for his pleasures, but he knew that she had to be taught a lesson now. It was time to show her that he really owned her, and it was time to punish her for her actions and prove to her that he was the boss and that she had no choice but to obey his every command. It was time to break her.

He was glad to have his backpack back, but more importantly, he was glad that he had been able to catch her. It was time for him to stop being nice to her. She was nothing more than a sex slave, and he was going to treat her as one from now on.

Chapter 11

With no other leads to go on and her investigation stalled, April sat at her desk and once again went over all of her evidence and reports. Something had to pop. Maybe she was overlooking some small fact or not looking at a piece of evidence in the right way. It was frustrating, and it was Amanda Webb that was suffering worse for it.

Amanda woke up on her bed again, and immediately felt the chains on her wrist and ankle. Her head ached and she felt dirty and grimy as she lay on the dirty sheets. She no longer cared if she was dirty, she felt alone and abandoned, and tears began to flow from her eyes once again. She had managed to escape but had made some poor choices after that and had gotten herself caught again. Why didn't she use that gun she found in the backpack? She could have ended this nightmare then, but she knew that she just could not kill another person.

Her love for humanity had now placed her in greater peril, and she was the only one that was going to pay a price for it. Something inside of her began to change at that moment, and she felt it. She felt anger now, she felt a will to survive, and a will to do whatever it took to survive. She wondered why the police had not come for her. She had purposely left her cell in the car with her purse, and she had taken pictures of her captor and his van, so where were the police? She moaned as she lay on the bed, then drifted off to sleep again.

Having calmed down and given the matter more thought, he decided that she needed to be taught a lesson. He had to break her will to ever try to escape. He recalled his days as a youth living with his step father and brother. His step father was a mean, and cruel drunk, and he had taken out his frustrations on him and his step brother many times with a belt. He learned to obey him quickly or suffer his wrath, and the belt was the reason why.

He stood up and walked into her room, then closed the door

behind him and stood still as he stared at Amanda. She had been sleeping, and the redness on her cheeks told him that she had been crying as well. She sat back on the bed and grabbed her pillow, pulling it tight against her chest, and he pointed at her and said, "It's time you learn a thing or two. I am your master. You will do my bidding. I own you, and you are like a dog to me. You will never leave here, got that?" She did not respond, and this angered him as he removed his belt and wrapped the end on his fist.

She gasped as he said, "I asked you a question, and you will respond." She nodded profusely and said, "Yes, I understand. I'm sorry for what I did." He had a wicked grin on his face as he began walking towards her, then he said, "You just lied to me, and I don't like it." He began striking her with the belt as she covered herself with the pillow, then he grabbed it and threw it on the floor, then began striking her with the belt again. He hit her on her arms, shoulders and head, as she laid on the bed screaming loudly, and he beat her body hard with the leather strap for minutes as he yelled out curses at her.

He growled loudly with each stroke of the belt, and he heard her screams. Within seconds of the beating he saw the red welts forming on her body, and the blood coming from them, then he finally let up and stood back and looked down at her as he breathed heavily. She was wailing as she lay in the fetal position, and his chest was heaving from the exertion, then he said, "You are lucky this time. If you ever try anything again I will torture you to death. Got it? You are mine and you will obey me!" He turned and left, locking the door behind him.

He was still angry as he went to get himself cleaned up. He felt that he had taught her a good lesson, and now he would have to give her some time to heal her body before he could take her. That thought angered him even more, but he knew that what he had just done was necessary to break her will, and he knew that from now on she would obey him out of fear. He went to the refrigerator and grabbed a cold beer and popped it open, then drained it in two large gulps.

He paced around the living room as he thought about Amanda and drank another beer. He did not want to have to beat her, but, just like the old woman he had to kill, she deserved to be punished. It wasn't his fault that she tried to escape. She would have brought the cops on him had he not caught her, so she got what she deserved. Feeling angry still, he decided to head out and fix the lock on her door then go to Pencil Bluff. After making sure that she could get out of the room, he grabbed the backpack, got in the van, then took off. He was going to grab more money, and if those rich people didn't cooperate, well, that was going to be their problem, not his. He was tired of living paycheck to paycheck, and now that he had another mouth to feed he would need more money. No more being Mr. nice guy he thought.

As he drove and thought about his situation, it came to him that he didn't really need to provide for another person. Why bother? He could just take a woman, use her for his pleasure, then get rid of her and take another one. He slammed his hand on the steering wheel and spoke aloud, "Yeah! That's the way to do it! He had seen two women go into that fancy RV, and one kinda looked young from a distance. Maybe it was the daughter. That meant attaching another chain to the wall, but he had plenty of spare chain in the shed. Still, he wanted to have more cash on hand and this was an easy way to get it.

He looked down at his speedometer and saw that he was going too fast, then brought his speed back under the limit again. He had not thought straight again and cursed himself for not staying sharp.

April heard from Amanda's family again. They were desperate to find her, and she felt terrible having to explain to them that, although they had made some progress, the truth was that they still had no clue where she was at or if she was still alive. The video and photographs she had turned into the FBI had not been able to provide any further clues, and the DNA found had not matched any known criminals. They still did not have a clear picture of the man who had stood in front of Amanda's car that fateful night, nor did they have a plate number on the vehicle.

The media had her story and picture on the screen but no one had called in a crime tip of any kind. April felt frustrated and wanted to find Amanda, but she was going to need some kind of a break in the case because right now she was backed up against a wall.

The van entered the town of Pencil Bluff, then it made its way to the rear of the RV Resort. He parked in a wooded area behind the resort after finding it on his map, and figured that he had about a half mile hike into the back of the property. The van was now hidden in the woods, so he took a heading and began to mark his trail by placing tissues on tree limbs, securing them with zip ties. He had to find his way back fast, especially if he had someone with him, then he was going to have to leave the area in a hurry.

He remembered that the fancy RV was parked across from another camper, and to the right of that were two more motor homes that were further down the gravel street. He did have some privacy, but not enough to make him comfortable. He also had to deal with any noises that the inhabitants may make. He had to get in fast without any of the neighbors seeing him, so he came up with an idea that would get the RV owners to let their guard down. He knew that people who camped were often very friendly to one another, so he was going to use that generosity to get himself inside that motor home.

He walked through the woods marking his way slowly, waiting for the evening to arrive. He figured that he still had about two or so hours of daylight left, so he had to make this quick to be able to find his way back through the woods while he still had some daylight. Finally reaching the rear area of the resort, he stopped in the woods and looked out through the trees, then found the motor home he was looking for. It had a screen door open, so he knew that the owners were inside.

Proceeding slowly out of the woods, he held his pistol underneath his map and looked around as he approached the motor home. No one else was outside now, so he hurried his steps and approached the screen door, then tapped lightly on it as he lowered his voice and said, "Hello neighbors!" A moment later the older woman appeared in the doorway and smiled back at him and said, "Hello there, are you lost?" She laughed since she saw him holding a map in front of him. He laughed back and said, "I just arrived and took one of the sites nearby. I was wondering if maybe you could help me. I saw your screen door open and I hope that you are a bit familiar with the area."

The woman smiled and said, "Well, I can try. "We've only been here a few days ourselves. What is it you're looking for?" She opened the screen door and he stepped forward, turning his map towards her. The second she looked down at it he took the two steps up, shoved her backwards, and was inside the motor home a second later, and his pistol was pointed in her face. She stepped back and gasped as her hand went to her mouth, then he said, "Make one sound and everyone in here dies. Move back."

She stepped back and he saw another woman coming from the rear of the coach, then he said, "Come over here and keep quiet or I drop her where she stands. Now!" He was instantly disappointed when he saw that she was not young. The woman obeyed and gasped also as she came forward. He said, "Who else is here?" The older woman said, "Just us, please, don't hurt us!" He said, "Both of you on the couch." Because he did not have his gloves on he used his foot to close the door and stepped forward as he removed his backpack. The younger woman began to cry now as she saw him remove rubber gloves from it and put them on, then take out a taser. Really fearing for their lives, the older woman pleaded with him again and he told them both to keep quiet.

He looked around the fancy motor home and was impressed. They had to have some serious cash. Maybe there was a young girl there and they were lying to protect her. He said, "Here's the deal. I want your money. All of it. Again I want to know if there is anyone else here. If you lie to me one of you dies now. I will tie you up and leave you in the back before I leave if you cooperate. If you don't, like I said, one of you dies." They had not thought that, since they had seen his face, there was no way that he was going to let them live. He pointed to the older woman and said, "Who's that woman to you?" She said, "She's my younger sister. Please mister, we'll give you the money, just don't hurt us, please! There is no one else here." Both of them had tears coming out of their eyes now, then he pointed to the older woman and said, "If you want your sister to live, go and get me all of the money. I'm gonna search the place after I tie you up so if I find that you held out on me she dies, and if you try anything stupid, she dies first."

He pointed at her with his pistol to get up, then she went to the back of the RV as he watched. He saw her open a closet and take her purse out, then she came back with it and set it on a table by the couch. She said, "It's all there. We keep most of the money in the bank, but please take it and leave, please." He said, "Put the cash on the table." She dug through the purse and pulled a wallet out, then took a thick stack of bills out and set it on the table. He said, "That's it? Remember that if I find any more your sister dies." She nodded and said, "I swear to you that this is all we have. We keep our money in the bank."

He said, "Count it." It totaled six hundred thirty dollars, and he became really angry. Not only did he not get a large sum like he had hoped for, but the younger woman he had seen from a distance turned out not to be as young as he had first thought. The younger sister had to be in her early fifties, and he had first thought that she was the old woman's daughter. He held the taser in his hand as they looked up at him, then he said, "Both of you lay flat on the floor face down."

The two women were still crying as they obeyed and took to the floor, then he bent down over them and held his knife with one hand as he grabbed the younger of the two by her hair and pulled her neck up off the floor. He hit the older woman with the taser first, then he placed the knife on her sister's throat and quickly slid it across it as the older woman began to scream and convulse form the 50,000 volts coursing through her body. Now he grabbed the older woman by the back of the hair and slammed her face on the floor, then lifted her neck and cut her throat open and stood up. He watched as both women kicked out violently as they struggled to breathe and blood poured out on the floor of the fancy motor home.

He could hear the gurgling sounds coming from their throats as their hands went to their throats hoping to somehow be able to breathe. Their bodies jerked on the floor for a few moments as they both continued to kick out with their feet, then they both stopped struggling and their arms went limp at their sides. He grabbed the cash and placed it in the backpack along with the taser, then he wiped the knife on a kitchen towel before placing it inside the pack. He took a quick walk to the rear bedroom and looked inside the closet, then he opened the dresser drawers and looked in them.

He saw another purse on the floor next to one of the nightstands and grabbed it. He found a wallet in it with about forty some dollars in it, so he took the cash and threw the purse down. He walked out past the lifeless bodies, put the backpack on and looked outside before stepping out. Still no one around, he closed the door behind him and removed the gloves, shoving then into his pocket, then headed to the back of the RV and into the wood line. A quick glance back before he left to make sure that he had not been seen, then he stepped into the woods and began his hike back.

He made good time back to the van then pulled out of the woods and onto the paved road, then made his way back to the main road and headed out. Although he had not made a big haul, still having the extra cash was going to make life easier on him. He drove the speed limit even though he felt like tearing out of the area because he felt the real fear of getting caught, telling himself that no one was going to find the bodies until tomorrow or maybe even later than that. His breathing finally returned to normal and he calmed down as he headed back home, then he began thinking about Amanda again. With all the cash he had now he was going to make another delivery with his fish and get paid, then he was going to tell his customers that he was retiring.

He was done fishing for a living. From now on he was going to prey on the elderly and live off of them. He made more money now by stealing from them, and he believed that if he planned things right he would end up with a nice load of cash and never get caught as long as he didn't leave any witnesses around. The more he thought about it, the more sense it made that he had made the right decision. Once he got home he was going to work on adding another set of chains though, because he was going out to find himself another young woman. Now that he had a good chunk of cash he could stay home for a good while and enjoy himself with Amanda and whoever else he would find and bring home.

There was no reason why he could not stretch his cash out as long as he did not need to keep a woman for a real long time and provide for her. Afterall, there were a lot of young girls to be had, and a lot of old people to provide a good living for him.

Chapter 12

It took two days before the Garland County Sheriff Department was called in to the Sunny Days RV Resort in Pencil Bluff. Amanda arrived after her crime scene unit and several deputies, then she went inside the motor home and saw the two bodies on the floor. Their blood had run all over the floor and was thick as it had begun to dry up. Deputy Young had been the first to respond at the scene, and April said, "What do we have Sonya?"

Sonya read from her notes, "Two females, Karen Potter and her sister Robin. A neighbor named Sylvia San Mateo called it in. She had a date set up to go hiking with them early this morning so she came over and knocked. She knew that they were home because their car is still parked in front of the motor home, so she knocked for at least ten minutes. She became worried and got the park manager, who also tried to knock for a few minutes. They decided to call it in. I arrived at the scene at seven thirty eight this morning and found the main entry door unlocked. The second I stepped inside I saw the blood, then the two bodies and called it in. I saw the open purse on the table and the wallet beside it, and it was open and empty. No one in the immediate area saw or heard anything and the only security cameras at the resort are at the pool and front gate."

The crime scene techs were busy checking for prints and DNA as the county ME (Medical Examiner), Dr. Peter Gustafson, was bent over the bodies examining them both. He looked up and said, "Hey there Detective Sanchez. Both ladies had their throats cut deeply and suffocated. So far I would say that time of death was at least 24 hours ago. I'll get a better idea when I perform the autopsy on them." April said, "Thanks Doc, I'm going to have a look around as soon as your people finish up. Any signs of a struggle or anything else visible on them?" He nodded no at her and resumed his investigation for a few moments longer, then he stood up and said, "I'll get to work on them as soon as they get to my lab. I should have the autopsy report to you by the end of the day or early tomorrow morning."

April waited until the crime scene unit finished up with their work, but in the meantime she told Deputy Young to send a deputy to the manager's office and get the video tape they had. She walked into the bedroom and saw that the closet door was open, as well as several drawers from the main dresser. She had seen the technician carry another purse out once he had bagged it, so she hoped that they would be able to get some finger prints from it. She searched the rest of the motor home but did not find anything of interest, then she stepped outside and spoke with Deputy Young again.

Deputy Young had already set up a perimeter around the motor home with the yellow crime scene tape, so April told her to let the manager know that no one was to disturb the area at all as she began to walk around the motorhome. The owner's car was still there and no one had seen or heard anyone or anything. She knew that the only security cameras were at other locations, and she saw the gravel road that led all around the resort. No way was she going to be able to get any tire prints off that. She stood and looked back at the RV and thought that if someone had driven here they would have had to park by the RV or near it, then she saw the trees above the large RV that stood tall behind it.

She walked back to the tree line and stopped to look around, then she gasped as she saw a set of footprints heading into the tree line. The prints were identical to the ones at the scene of Amanda's kidnapping. She called her crime scene unit back there right away, then left a deputy to point them out to them while she and Deputy Young took to the woods. Several feet into the forest they spotted the zip tie marking, then spotted another and began to follow them. She saw the same prints again when she approached a soft spot of dirt, then called for a tech to come there while they waited to get more photographs of the footprints and the zip ties with tissue marking a trail.

It took eight minutes for the tech to get to her location, then she and Deputy Young continued following the zip tie markers.

She instructed the tech to gather all of them after photographing them, then she and her deputy followed them until they ended up in a small clearing. Deputy Young stooped down and pointed to the ground as she said, "We have tire treads here." April looked closely at them and shook her head as she said, "Both the tire and footprints are exactly the same as the ones by Amanda Webb's car. We have the same person doing both crimes Sonya. I bet that any DNA they get from the RV will match."

She could not believe this. How was it that this same guy ended up here of all places. Why here and why that RV? Did the two murdered women know who he was? Maybe the park video would reveal information. She saw the tire markings as they headed out to the paved road, then the dirt marking as the van made a left turn on it. All of those marks would be inspected by crime scene people, but she had to get ahold of the video and look at it now. She called the deputy that had gone to retrieve it and asked him to wait by her car as they made their way back to it, then put patrols in the area to see if they could spot the van.

April then headed back to the manager's office and asked him if they held on to recordings for a certain period of time. He said, "Don't need to. The equipment we use allow us to store them in the cloud, then they are held there for thirty days unless we move it to a file. We've always let them expire thirty days later since there was never a need to keep them around any longer." She said, "So, since today is the fourteenth, that means that right now I can actually see video recording all the way back to the first of the month correct? He said she could, then he created a file and downloaded them into it, then he emailed it to her as she stood there. She thanked him, gave him her business card and told him that if anyone told him they had seen anything at all to call her, then she headed back to the station.

She hoped that she was going to be able to spot the van in one of those videos, but more importantly, its driver. It made no sense to her that he had traveled here to commit a double murder and rob the two ladies. She had no idea how much money he had taken, but she saw that he had not stolen any jewelry or electronics, just money. Mrs. Richards had been killed and her family had confirmed that she had always kept cash in the shoebox, and now the two dead women's purses had their wallets emptied. It seemed that the killer was going after seniors to rob them, and he planned on not leaving any witnesses to identify him afterwards.

Still no sign of Amanda, and she was young. How did she fit into the picture? Did he take her to kill or to have around to sexually abuse her? Then, if he did, was he planning on killing her also? She had to find the young woman and hoped that she was still alive. There had to be something that she was missing, and she believed that it still had to do with the van.

This was the last time he had to collect his trot lines, and it felt strange as he hauled his catch in. He ended up with a decent haul this time, so maybe his luck was changing. He prepared his catch, placing them on ice in the large plastic bins he carried in the back of the van, then he headed back home to check on Amanda before he left to make his last delivery ever.

After entering her room he saw that she was lying on the bed still, and she was quiet. Her back was turned to him, so he said, "How are you feeling? I got some lotion here. When I get back from doing my last delivery we'll get you cleaned up. You need to put on clean clothes and I'll throw them sheets in the wash. Hungry or thirsty?" No answer, so he asked again. Still no response, so he walked to the other side of the bed and looked at her.

She was sleeping, so he went and fetched a bottle of water and set it on her nightstand, then he locked the room and left. When he got back he would get her up, clean her up, then put some medicine on her. Once he finished with that he would make sure that she ate and drank. He wanted her to heal as soon as possible so that he could have her and enjoy himself. As he locked the gate behind him and got back into the van he thought about how long he was going to keep her around.

As he drove into town he decided that how long he kept her

would depend on how fast she recovered and how good a time he was going to have with her. There were plenty of other young girls to be had, and all he had to do was to take one from someplace farther away. He had his delivery to make now, then he was going to stay home for a few weeks and just enjoy his time with Amanda while the cops ran around trying to figure out who had killed the two women at the trailer park place. His customers were going to ask why he was stopping deliveries, and his answer was simple. He was going to tell them that he had to leave the state to take care of his dying father in Minnesota. Maybe they would feel sorry for him and pay him extra. He had to make sure that they all heard him tell them that he was leaving the state for good tomorrow.

A few more good hauls of cash would allow him to live a better life, a life of nothing but pure joy with his woman and the new ones he would bring home later on. He looked at the cash he had collected as it sat on his front passenger seat and smiled. Coupled with his cash he had stolen, he felt real proud of himself because he had never had that much money before, and it felt really good. He confirmed in his mind that he was now on the right track for sure, and that was to take cash from the old people and enjoy his life from now on.

Chapter 13

Amanda had heard every word he had said to her. She chose to fake sleep so that she would not have to talk to him or look at him. He had hurt her pretty bad. Her whole body ached and felt like it was on fire. It hurt each time she moved, and some of the welts were deep enough to bleed. She saw the blood stains on the sheets but did not care. She felt completely helpless and afraid as she thought about her family and friends. They would all be worried for her, and her new boyfriend would really feel terrible. She missed them all and, she wanted desperately to see them all again.

There was only one person to blame for all of this, and that was the man who had kidnapped her. She knew that in another day or two he was going to come for her, and she would not be able to stop him. Just thinking about it made her want to throw up, but she knew that unless she did something to help herself soon she was going to die here and no one would ever find her. She finished crying and stood up, then she tried the lock as she looked at the door. He had repaired it, but she could see where it was cracked from when he broke it down. Maybe if she found a way to pop the lock on it she may be able to get it open. But the chains on her leg and arm would still be there. The only key to her chains and door was with him, and he was not going to repeat the mistake of having them hanging on his side any longer.

She had more thinking to do before he returned. She had to figure out a way to get away from this place. She was going to say another prayer but decided not to since it had not done any good so far. She felt the anger inside of her and knew that this ordeal had changed her forever. The next time that she was going to escape was going to be her last because she decided that she was not coming back to this living hell again. She also knew that if she would be able to get her hands on that gun again she would not hesitate to use it. She knew that she was now a different person than before she had been brought here.

April was back at her desk going through the video recording from the RV Resort. She had finished the first week already and started on week two. She couldn't help feeling a little deflated as she had thus far not seen any white vans show up, but she kept going through them. Another day from the video passed by with no results, then she sat up on her chair as she saw a white van enter through the front entrance. It rolled straight through as though it belonged there, and she could only see the side of it and not the license plate. She waited then saw it again as it now appeared to be in the parking lot by the swimming pool. It stopped there and just waited, but the driver did not get out.

She said, "Come on out you rat, come on out!" She waited for him to come out of the van but instead she saw a group of people leaving the pool. She looked at them in slow motion, then she spotted the two Potter sisters as they walked among the group. A few moments later she saw the van slowly move out and fol-low behind them before it disappeared out of the camera's view all together. So that was how he had come to kill those two women. He saw them at the pool and followed them, then he had to see the new and expensive coach where they lived. He was after them because he believed that they had to be rich.

April ran the tape through five more times as she tried to see any details she had not seen the first time. Now she saw the en-tire van, and she saw the dent on the rear passenger side quarter panel also. Still not able to get the plate number, she was able to see that the driver was wearing a white cowboy hat after she slowed the video even more. She emailed the tape to Special Agent Foster at the FBI with a note asking her to see if the FACE Services Unit could do some magic on it. She ran the rest of the tapes and never saw the van again, but now she knew that he had gone there to scout around and find a target to hit.

This made her wonder why there. He had to have known that this place existed somehow. The resort was in a somewhat rural area, and not off a main road. He had to have known about it be-fore. Had he camped there himself? What ties did he have to this place? She grabbed the phone and called the resort, then asked the manager if he was aware of any companies that had vans that perhaps had done work on the property. He mentioned that, other than the electric or phone company, at times vans made deliveries to the resort. He had no regular business that came in on a scheduled call, and he did not recognize the white van at all.

He knew what everyone staying there drove, even if they towed it behind a motorhome. After checking his log he confirmed that no current resident listed a van at the resort. Still, the killer drove in like he knew where to go, then he drove out the front gate again. April said, "If you can, please check to see if any companies came to your place to do any work there in the past month or so. I need to see if I can identify the white van or its driver." He told her he would check and call if he found something, then she hung up and called Sheriff Thomas to let him know what she had found.

The sheriff listened quietly, then he said, "Sounds to me that you're on the right track. We know now that the guy who kidnapped Amanda and killed Dolores Richards is the same one that killed the Potter sisters. I suspect that the DNA evidence from this crime scene will be a match to prove it. I still believe that it was he who killed the Richards lady since we saw the white van passing by her home on that video. Your theory of him robbing older people also makes sense. He figures that they are easy targets and must have money, then he kills them so that they can't identify him. I need to issue a warning to our senior citizens, in the meantime please let me know what else you find out from here April, good job."

This haul of fish had netted him over $250 dollars. He felt happy knowing that never again would he have to deal with the weather to make a living, and from now on he was going to make even more money. He stopped to top the gas tank off, then picked up a case of beer to celebrate once he got home. He still had to get Amanda cleaned up and wash her bed sheets and clothes, but in another day or two he was going to be in paradise because she was a really hot girl.

He parked the van in front of the shed and emptied the containers he used to haul his catch, then he took everything out related to his fishing business and put it all away in the shed. He smiled as he parked the van in front of the house now, picked up his beer and snacks, and went inside the house. He decided to get started cleaning Amanda up and do some laundry, so he entered her room and stood by the door and saw that she was sitting on the edge of the bed. He looked at her and saw a different look in her face. She seemed to be looking through him, not at him, and he felt uncomfortable. He cleared his throat first, then said, "We need to get you showered. I put lotion on the sink and some women's shampoo in the shower. I want you to put the clothes on that I left in the bathroom for you when you finish, got it?" She nodded.

He said, "Um, well, yeah, also I'll get the sheets off the bed and wash them. When you get cleaned up I'll make us something to eat and I expect you to eat. While you are in the bathroom I will standing guard outside the door because you can't be trusted. Now, I want you to take a look at what I'm holding here. That's right, it's a taser, and it will zap your butt real good if you try something stupid. I will chain you up again when you get cleaned up. Oh, the bathroom window is just glass block so there's no way out of there, let's go."

He unlocked her chain while holding the taser close to her, then he led her into the hallway and had her enter the bathroom. He said, "I'll be right here waiting."

Amanda closed the door and saw a large towel draped over the sink next to a bottle of lotion, then she looked at the shower and saw soap and shampoo. She turned the water on and stripped off her clothes carefully, then she entered the shower and began to clean herself up. At times, the pressure of the water hurt when it fell on one her welts, but eventually she got used to it and finished her shower. She saw a new t-shirt and shorts and underwear on top of the toilet, then saw a pair of socks next to them and began putting lotion on her body.

It felt good on her body, and now that she had a mirror she began to examine herself closely. She saw that she had lost weight and that she had dark spots under her eyes from lack of sleep and worry. The clothes felt loose on her body but she was glad to be wearing clean clothes again. Next to the sink she saw a basket with toiletries in it, and they were still in the wrappers. New toothpaste and a new toothbrush, a brush and some deodorant made her feel a little better, but her thoughts were consumed with her captor. For the first time in her life she felt anger and hatred, and all that she could think about was getting away from the monster who had brought her there.

He waited for a whole hour before the bathroom door opened, and he smiled at her as she came out. She looked a lot better now, and he hoped that her wounds were healing good. He held the taser out and said, "Back in your room." He told her to stand after he hooked the chains back on her, then he removed the bed and pillow sheets and threw them in the wash. He told her that he was going to make something to eat while the laundry was being done, then he locked the door again.

He had dinner ready and the laundry hanging outside to dry, so he took the food into her room and said, "Just hold on, I got some things for you." He left then returned carrying a small table and a chair, then he left again and came back with a large bag in his hand. He dumped the items on the bed and said, "Here's some magazines and some snacks for you. This new antenna here will work better. I'll get it hooked up for you." Amanda watched him hook it up and try it, and she saw that she was now able to get some local channels. He said, "I'll get the sheets for you and you can put them on the bed."

By the time she had eaten and replaced her sheets he seemed pleased about it, but she was seething inside. He believed that she should be real happy about her situation now, never thinking that she was there against her will, nor caring that she was not going to see her family anymore. Those thoughts never entered his head. She turned the local news on and began to watch it, then she saw the Garland County Sheriff warning senior citizens to be sure they locked their doors and not to travel anywhere alone. She saw a picture of the van on the screen and heard that the driver was wanted by police for murder and kidnapping.

She shook her head slowly as she watched, then she saw a picture of herself on the screen and gasped. Before she knew it she saw her parents on the screen as they begged for the kidnapper to let her go free. She began to cry then as her hands went to her face, and she looked at her door, then at her chains again. She had to get away. The coverage ended and a commercial came on, and she glanced at the screen as she stood to turn the TV off, but just then she saw that it was about a candy bar, and how the husband did everything on his wife's to do list just so he could get a candy bar.

Now she knew how she was going to make her escape. She was going to convince him that she had turned and accepted her fate, that he had broken her will. She was going to gain his trust, then she was going to hurt him real bad. She felt her heart leap with joy now as she found a new inner strength, then she began to think of what she needed to do.

He was real happy. Amanda looked better cleaned up, and all the stuff he had got for her should make her happy. He saw the welts on her figured that in a couple of days she would be feeling a lot better, and so would he. Tomorrow he was going to check her wounds and see how they were healing, then he would know if he had to wait one or two more days before he took her for himself. He popped a cold beer and turned the television on, but after a few beers he drifted off to sleep on the couch.

Chapter 14

April had racked her brains trying to figure out the DMV report not listing the van owner that she was looking for. She had watched Sheriff Thomas warn the senior citizens about the killer, then when he had announced to them that he was increasing the patrols in the county. She felt the pressure of not being able to find the killer and wanted badly to figure out what it was that was bothering her about the report.

As she went through her notes again she kept thinking about the RV Resort. Why, out of all of the places to go, would this guy attack two women there? How did he know to go there in the first place. The Richards home where he had killed the old woman and robbed her was in Hot Springs Village, far away from the RV resort. She knew that if she could figure that out she would find this guy. As she was getting her second cup of coffee a thought came to her, and she rushed back to her desk and called the manager at the RV Resort again. She had to wait a few minutes because he was out in the park, but when he came on the phone April said, "Find anything out for me about any companies that came there to do service or maybe even a delivery?"

The manager said, "No, and I went through the records all the way back to a year and a half ago. That was when I was hired here. The old manager retired and I came on board then. I keep really good record Detective Sanchez, and I'm sorry but, other than the phone or electric company, there hasn't been any other white vans doing business here." April said, "I was going to ask you to check further back, but if there are no records available I guess I can scrap that idea." He said, "Well no, there aren't any records from before I came to work here. The old manager wasn't that efficient. But, he retired and has a trailer here, so maybe I can ask him if he knows anything about a white van. He may be old, but he has a sharp memory. He can still name people that visited here as far back as ten years ago!"

April thanked him and hung up, then she started looking up

the names of every retirement community in the county. She figured that, other than Hot Springs Village, he may hit one of those places next time. She found six other places besides the Village, where people 55 plus lived at, then she called Sheriff Thomas and asked for increased patrols in those communities. He agreed and told her that it was a great idea, then she said, "One more thing Sheriff. He has to eat and get gas somewhere. I think that we should post flyers at the grocery stores and at every gas pump in the county for people to be on the lookout for a white van with dent in the rear passenger side, and asking them to call 911 and not approach it. I can use our young people in the Explorer Program to distribute them and not take up any deputy's time to do that."

The sheriff liked that idea as well and gave her a thumbs up, then she contacted Deputy April Sanders who ran the Explorers Program to get her help. The program allowed students in high school who had an interest in law enforcement to join and learn all about becoming a deputy as they got involved in community service matters, traffic control, and many other department functions. The students participated in exercising, and learned firearm safety as well as first aid. She knew that they would all be eager to help and distribute the flyers, and maybe it would help and someone would spot the van and call it in.

April was trying to do anything she could to find the killer, but she wanted more than anything to find Amanda Webb, really hoping that she was still alive. She picked up the DMV report and began going over it again hoping that something would catch her eye that she had missed before.

He woke up on the couch with drool coming out his mouth, then he stood up and saw that he had to clean up his empty beer cans. After a bathroom break he made some coffee and ate, then he cleaned up before going into Amanda's room with some food for her. He no longer gave her anything that she could use as a weapon against him, so he had bought her plastic bottles of milk and juice to drink. He left her food on the table and told her that he would return in an hour for the tray. He noticed that she was finally starting to treat him better. That beating he gave her must have done some good he thought.

Amanda was awake and sitting at the table when he came in with the tray of food. She began working her plan right away by smiling and thanking him for the food, then she ate as soon as he left. She knew that he was going to ask about her wounds, so she had to stall him some more to make sure that he didn't feel that it was time for him to take her, so she began thinking about what to tell him as she thought about her escape. She was going to ask him to take her outside to get some sunshine, so she had to butter him up first. Her plan was to familiarize herself with the outside of the home so that she could see where it was best for her to go the next time she got out of there, and her plan was to get out of there real soon.

She nodded slowly as she finished eating and set the empty juice jar on the tray. Right in front of her was her way out, but first she wanted to get a look outside. Before she realized it, the door was being unlocked and he stepped inside the room. She no longer saw the key ring hanging on his side, but she had seen him go into his right pocket to get it out when he left the room. He walked up and grabbed the plastic tray, then Amanda faked a smile and said, "Thank you for the food, and for letting me get cleaned up. I can see why you said that you're not a bad guy. Even though you hit me with your belt, I understand why. I deserved it, and I'm sorry for not trusting you, it's just that I was afraid."

He said, "Like I told you, I don't want to hurt you, but I can't have you trying to leave. How are you feeling?" She rubbed her shoulder and said, "A little better. Some of the welts are still real sore and it hurts if I sit or lay on them. I think that they should be better in about four or five days though." She saw the look of surprise on his face as she said that, then he said, "Well, put more lotion on them cause I ain't about to wait no more than two more days. I aim to enjoy myself with you then, and it would be real good for you if you go along with it. I can be real nice if you treat me right."

Amanda said, "I understand. I think that some sun will really help my body a lot. If you keep the chains on me will you allow me to sit outside on the porch? I promise that I will behave. The more sunshine I get the faster I will heal." He shook his head slightly and she knew that it had worked, then he said, "I'll rig up a new chain to use. This is what I want to see and hear from you. You'll see that being here ain't that bad at all." She watched him dig the key out of his right pocket again as he left and locked the door.

It was working well, and she felt that she could make him let his guard down again. Now that she knew he would wait no longer than two more days, she had to be prepared to put a plan into action that would work. She knew that there was no way she wanted that monster to have sex with her at all, and she would rather die than allow him to rape her.

He was really pleased as he left the room. She was finally breaking, and soon would be his. He went to the shed and cut a piece of chain ten feet long, then attached another shackle to it. He would use one of the locks on her chain now to lock her ankle to it, but he was going to carry his taser with him. He had learned a lesson that she was not to be trusted, and he suspected that she may be pretending to be nice just so that she could try to get away again, but this time he was going to be ready. He was going to let her go out and let the sunshine heal her body, but he was going to make her strip tomorrow so that he could take a look at it himself.

If it looked OK tomorrow, he would take her then, but he was not about to wait any more than two days. The chain made, he went back and secured it on her other ankle before he removed the other chains, then he held the taser as he held the other end of the chain in the other hand. He led her out the back door of the house and had her sit on the step, then he said, "The morning sun is always out back here. In the afternoon you can go up front." He sat on a rocking chair holding the chain and watched her. Although he knew that she could not escape, he enjoyed looking at her body.

He had never had a girlfriend after high school, and he had only been with a woman one time when his brother paid for a prostitute to have sex with him. He remembered that he had watched them and he did not like it, but he had told him that since he had paid for it he was going to watch, so he had no choice. Other than that one time, he had not been with a woman at all since then. He decided then that even if she wasn't fully healed tomorrow, he was not waiting any longer than that. He felt the excitement again as he stared at her.

Amanda turned and smiled at him, then thanked him again for bringing her outside. She saw the way that he was staring at her and she became frightened and looked away. He looked like a hungry predator about to strike, and she began to rethink her plan as she studied the area in the back of the house. She had looked quickly at the front door as she passed by through the hallway, and she had not seen the backpack laying by it, so she wondered where he was keeping it now. She was going to need to find it to get that gun he had. At least she knew that he had lied to her about having mean dogs outside. She believed that he had some mental issues, maybe even having multiple personalities. She wondered if he felt fear when he watched the news and saw that the police were looking for him.

The sun shifted to the front of the home, and he led her back inside to make some lunch. She turned the news on and watched, but there was nothing new on it concerning her captor. She believed that he was the one that had robbed and killed those elderly women, and she knew that he was far more dangerous than she first thought he was. One mistake and she would find herself in a real bad situation, so she had to make sure that her plan to escape would work. She had come up with a simple plan, and after seeing him staring at her, she believed that he was not going to wait too much longer before he would rape her. She decided to put her plan into action tomorrow. If it worked she would be free, and if it failed she would die tomorrow.

He did not come back to allow her to go out on the front porch, and she did not see him again until he brought her a tray of food for the night. As difficult as it was, she forced herself to thank him, to smile and him, and to ask if he would allow her outside again tomorrow. His answer frightened her when he said, "Yeah, I figure that we will take a close look at you tomorrow and see how you're healing. Use the lotion again and get some rest." He closed the door and locked it, and she knew then that he was not going to wait any longer than tomorrow to force himself on her, especially after seeing the wicked grin on his face.

She felt fear as she thought that tomorrow might very well be her last day alive, but then the fear was replaced with anger as she thought of how he had taken her, then beaten her, and now was about to begin using her for his own sick pleasure. She became more determined now to put an end to this madness tomorrow, no matter the outcome. That night she slept better than she had since being brought here against her will.

Chapter 15

Detective Sanchez looked over the photographs and videos once again. She had just arrived at work and had filled her mug with hot coffee, then she got started going through them because she was trying to see if she could catch one small detail that may help her identify the killer. Her photos had been enhanced by the FBI's FACE Services Unit, and she now had a clearer view of the man wearing the white cowboy hat. She saw that he wore a beard of dark color, brown or black, and she knew that he was approximately six feet tall and weighed around 200 pounds, but his face was not completely clear in the photo. With no license plate information available it made it difficult to identify the owner of the van though, then her phone rang.

The RV Resort manager was on the line, and he said, "Detective Sanchez I was able to speak with Walter. He's the one I told you about before that used to manage the park here. He seemed to recall a white van that had made a delivery here, but he said that it was years ago and that he had nothing to do with it. Apparently a group of full time campers had decided to throw a celebration on their own to celebrate somebody's birthday, so they decided to have a load of fish delivered. He remembered it because one of the women from that group asked him to keep his eye out for the delivery van and guide it to the swimming pool area where the fish fry was to occur."

April felt a tinge of hope and said, "Go on." Well, anyway, according to Walter, the van came to deliver a large order of fish, so he stopped it at the front entrance and had it follow him around back to the pool area. He watched the men deliver several crates of fresh fish, then they left. He never knew who they were he said because he had nothing to do with arranging the delivery in the first place, and as far as he remembers, the van did not have any kind of sign on it. It was just white."

April said, "OK, this is exactly what I am looking for. Any idea of the date when that occurred?" The manager said, "Walter can't recall, but he said that it was at least three or four years ago." Then April said, "Walter mentioned the men doing a delivery, so was there two or three? Can he recall that and hopefully what they looked like?" He laughed and said, "Yeah, he told me that he was kind of surprised to see these guys, two of them. He said they looked like hillbillies. Long hair, beards, and that they were big guys. They never spoke to anyone except when the women paid them and gave them a bonus for making a last minute delivery. One of them thanked them, then they left. He said he never saw the men or the van ever again."

April said, "Is there anyone living there still that was involved in the celebration?" He said, "Just one couple, they retired and live here full time still. The others moved on since then. If you want, I can arrange for you to meet with them." April thanked him, then said, "I need to speak with them right away, I'm on the way." She felt some excitement after that conversation as she rushed to her car. Hopefully the couple would provide more detailed information that would prove useful.

Last night was difficult for Amanda. It took her a few hours to fall asleep because she kept thinking about what may happen the next day. Her thoughts turned to her family, her boyfriend, and her friends as she thought that after tomorrow she may never see them again and they may never find out what had happened to her. She cried some, then went through a period of such fierce anger that it made it difficult for her to relax.

Before falling asleep her last thoughts were to be prepared to take action, because her monster was coming to inspect her body. If he believed that she had healed well enough, he would rape her for certain. She thought of what to try to tell him about her wounds to see if she could persuade him to wait another day, but what was the use? Either way she was going to be raped repeatedly either tomorrow or the next day at most, then from then on who knew how often it would happen after that.

It was her final thought before she drifted off to sleep that finally calmed her. The thought of going to war with this guy.

He was stronger and had all the advantages, but she was going to put up a fight for her freedom and give it her all. If he won, she would face being raped and probably killed, but staying here was not an option any longer.

When she awoke in the morning she immediately began going over her plan in her head. She kept it simple, and either it would work perfectly or it wouldn't. She sat at the table waiting as she watched the early morning news, then she heard the door unlocking.

He had woken up feeling excited. He knew that he was about to show Amanda why she had was brought here in the first place, and he couldn't wait. He prepared breakfast with eggs, bacon, juice and toast, then carried the tray into her room. He saw her at the table and she was smiling at him again, so he felt that maybe she would not be much of a problem. He set the tray down on the table and said, " I decided to make us something good to eat today. I want you to enjoy it. I'll come back for the tray in an hour, then we need to take a look at your bruises. Don't worry, all I want to do is to take a look."

He had lied to her so that she would not be afraid to strip her clothes off, and if she looked even remotely OK he was going to take her right then and there. It was time for her to understand her role. If she went along with it he would let her sit outside in the sunshine when they finished, if she fought him then he would take what he wanted, beat her to death, then take her into the woods out back and bury her. He wasn't going to put up with any problems from her especially since she had already tried to escape. He was coming in with his taser in hand, then make her strip in front of him as he watched. After that, he knew that he was going to take her one way or another. The more he thought about it, the more he convinced himself that today was the day. No more waiting he thought, as he felt himself getting excited once again.

Detective Sanchez had her light bar on as she rushed to the

resort, and with the light traffic on the road she made it there in forty five minutes. The park manager saw her enter the park and met her outside, then he got in the car with her and gave her directions to the couple's home. He knocked on their door and introduced April, then they were led to their living room. April briefly explained why she was there and asked what they could recall about the celebration and the two men that delivered the fish that day. She learned their names were Tom and Mattie Knott.

Mrs. Knott spoke first and said, "Yes, I remember that day. We had a nice cookout by the pool. We had a load of fresh fish delivered, yes." April waited but she did not continue, then Mr. Knott said, "Mattie is not well detective. I was there that day. In fact, I was the one who found them and asked them to deliver the fish. I remember that they told me no at first, so I offered them and extra hundred bucks if they came, and another fifty if they showed up the next day in the morning. That was the only way to get them to come, but they showed up."

Mattie said, "The fish was so delicious!" April smiled at her then looked at Tom and said, "How did you find those men, and did they have a white van?" He said, "Well, we were in Hot Springs Village a few days before that doing some shopping and we stopped at a restaurant to eat. Mattie loved the fish so much that she asked where they got it, and they told us that they have it delivered fresh from two men who fish for a living. They gave us their name and number, and for some reason I kept it. When the women decided to have that big fish fry Mattie here told them that we could get the fish delivered. They all pitched in, then I had to go back and tell them that if they wanted them delivered the next day it was gonna cost a hundred and fifty extra because the men told that they had to collect their trot lines, pack them in ice, then drive them to us. They were our only hope to get the fish, and yes, they drove a white van. They had these plastic crates in the back packed full of fish on ice."

April said, "Tell me, was this a company that delivered to you? Did you see a logo or a name on their van?" He looked at his wife and she shrugged her shoulders, then he said, "Not that I can recall. They didn't say much. They asked us where we wanted the fish, then said, thanks after I paid them. In and out, real quick." April said, "What did they look like? Were they tall, thin, heavy, any scars or tattoos on them that you recall?" He leaned back and rubbed his chin, then Mattie said, "They were scary looking."

April looked at her, then her husband said, I remember thinking that they reminded me of hillbillies. Both had hats, wore long, dark beards, and they smelled like fish. No scars or anything that I recall though, but they were tall." He stood up and said, "Just a minute and I'll get that phone number for you." April said, "You still have it?" He pointed to his wife and said, "Mattie wanted me to keep it in case she ever wanted to order again. Funny thing is though, I remember calling them maybe five, six months later and the man I spoke to told me that he was working alone now and only delivered to restaurants."

April said, "Can you tell me the name of the restaurant where you ate at and got their phone number Mr. Knott?" Mattie said, "It was blue!" April smiled again and looked at her husband as he thought about the name for a moment. He shook his head and said, "I can't remember since we never went back again. Like Mattie said though, it was painted blue and they were all about seafood. Mattie here loves seafood." April thanked them then dropped the manager off and thanked him, then she headed back to her office to look up restaurants in the Village. As many times that she had been all through the Village, she could not recall any seafood places there painted blue though.

She used the light bar in her car to hurry back. She now had a phone number to trace, so she called Sheriff Thomas and filled him in on what she had just discovered. He told her that he would get a court order and have the phone company trace the number, and April felt hope for the first time since she had begun her investigation. The names on the paper that Mr. Knott had given her were first names only, but now she knew that they fished for a living, owned a white van, and sold them locally. She called Special Agent Foster of the FBI and filled her in on her way back to the sub-station, and Sharon told her that she would get started looking up the restaurants in the Village in the meantime.

Things were finally happening in the right way and April hoped that she would find out what she needed to know, and that hopefully she would find Amanda soon after that.

Amanda ate quickly. She wanted to put some energy into her body in case she would have to run far, then she went over her plan in her head to be ready. About an hour later she heard the door being unlocked, and instinctively said a prayer. She felt ready, and did not feel any fear at all, which surprised her. She really had changed inside.

Chapter 16

He felt the rush. It was show time now. He grabbed the taser and walked down the hallway, then unlocked the door and stepped inside. She was sitting at the desk, and her food was all gone. Her smile caught him off guard because she knew that he was going to make her take her clothes off, yet here she was smiling at him. He recalled that she had fooled him once before, so he made sure that she saw the taser in his hand before he said, "Get enough to eat?"

Amanda nodded and said, "Yes, and thank you for cooking such a nice meal. I appreciate it." He nodded back, then said, "OK, it's time to have a look at your wounds. If everything goes well I'll let you go out on the front porch today." He realized then that he should not have said that because she may think that he was about to take her to bed, but her smile and friendly nod told him that she had not grasped that. He said, "OK, let me take the tray back to the kitchen, then you go over to the bed and show me the wounds."

Amanda smiled and said, "Fine, here you go." She stood, picked up the tray, making sure that it hung out over the table, then dropped it, making it look like an accident, then she gasped as she said, "Oh, sorry, I didn't mean to do that!" Without thinking, he just reacted and bent down to grab the tray with both hands, still holding the taser with part of his right hand, then at that moment Amanda turned, grabbed her chair, lifted it, then brought it crashing down as hard as she could on the back of his head. He dropped to the ground instantly and appeared to be out cold, so she rushed to his side and felt around in his right pocket for the keys. The moment her fingers touched them she felt elated, then she pulled them out and began to unlock her chains. In an instant she was free, then she grabbed the taser and ran out of the door.

She knew that the door was not going to hold him for long, but she locked it anyway, then ran into the living room. A quick look around and she did not see the keys to the van or the backpack, so she ran into what she hoped was his bedroom. The second she walked inside she smelled the foul stench from the room never being cleaned, but she saw the backpack lying on the floor next to his bed. She ran up to it and opened it, and there was the gun and a lot of cash, as well as some rope, duct tape, a box of ammunition, and plastic zip ties. She grabbed the pistol and checked it to make sure that it was loaded, then she looked around for a set of keys to the van but did not see them.

She knew that he would come to at any moment, so she ran out of the room without the keys to the van. She glanced back at her room and saw that the door was still shut, so she ran to the kitchen and threw a couple bottles of juice in the backpack from the refrigerator, then ran outside after donning the backpack. This time she held the gun in her hand, and she was about to use it. She ran to the van and pointed it at the front tire, then pulled the trigger. Nothing happened, and she was stunned. She felt herself panicking as she looked at it and she knew that she saw the magazine was fully loaded, but she did not understand why it would not fire.

Still panicking, she looked back at the house and still did not see or hear him, so she looked at the gun again as she tried to figure out why it would not fire. The safety. She looked for a safety, but she had no idea what it would look like. She tried to think what she was doing wrong, but her mind raced with fear. He would be coming for her any moment now. She yelled out, "Think Amanda! Think!" Suddenly she remembered a scene from a movie where she saw a police officer pull the gun back to load it, so she began pulling on the slide.

The first time she tried she had not pulled it far enough, so she pulled it backwards harder and it locked in the open position. Now what? She tried to push it forward again but couldn't, then she looked at the house again and back at the gun. She felt like crying, but she saw a piece on the side that seemed to be holding the gun in the open position. It had a small thumb catch on it, so she pressed it. Nothing happened, the gun would not go forward. She yelled out of fear and anger then as she pushed harder on the thumb catch, it suddenly popped closed in an instant. She heard and saw the bullet load, then she yelled out, "Yes!"

April stepped back, pointed the pistol at the tire, held it with both hands, then pulled the trigger. The loud boom made her jump backwards, but the tire deflated right away. She looked back again at the house, then took off running down the dirt road. This time he was going to have to catch her on foot, and this time she would use the gun if he came at her. She knew she still had the taser inside the backpack in case she had trouble with the gun, but for now all she could think of was to run as fast as possible. Never again was she going back to that house.

By the time April made it back to the station she got a call from Special Agent Foster. Sharon said, "The place you are looking for is out business April. It was called Village Seafood. I looked up an old picture of it and the building was painted blue just like the woman told you. However, I called a few other restaurants in town that serve seafood, and was told that one man delivers fresh fish to them twice a week. Got a name and a number. I ran the phone number through our system and found that it no longer exists. We will need to have the phone company run a trace on it to see who it belonged to. The restaurant manager gave me a description of the man and the van, and it's white. It gets even better, he confirmed that there is a dent on it. He told me that they guy lives by a creek that runs into the Ouachita River and has been fishing for a living for a lot of years."

April ran inside and rushed to her desk not believing the sudden good fortune thrown her way, then said, "We need to check with every restaurant serving seafood and see if anyone has an address for him." Sharon said, "I have people on it already and we will know in minutes, I'll call you back." April searched her laptop for the restaurants as she waited for a call back, then three minutes later her phone rang. She saw the caller ID letting her know that it was FBI, she grabbed the receiver and said, "Tell me you got it Sharon."

Sharon's excited voice came through as she said, "You're not going to believe this. The name is Will Feller, but everyone calls him Bear. Got an address too, but it's the same as the one we went to already. Remember the abandoned farm house out in that remote dirt road?" April stood and began to pace, then she said, "There's something we're missing here Sharon. It makes no sense. Feller is the name of the guy that went to prison. He died there. Why does this guy use that name and address?" Sharon said, "It's all some sort of glitch with that DMV report. The van it showed registered was to a man named Feller, and the address was to the abandoned farmhouse, but the vehicle registration is current."

April was listening as she thought, then it suddenly came to her. She yelled out, "Sharon, the registration is current but someone else must pay it. Someone that does not live at that address. I need to call the DMV again, in the meantime see if any of the restaurant employees know anything about where this Bear guy lives." April called the DMV and spoke to a supervisor, explaining the emergency situation to her. The supervisor said, "I can find out where the payment comes from, it should be in our system, hold on a second." It was the longest second that she ever experienced, but the supervisor came back on the line and said, "The payment comes from a law firm in Little Rock. Here's their name and address."

April looked up the law firm then called them. The receptionist did not seem to be interested that she had an emergency and placed her on hold, then moments later a man answered and said, "Attorney Mark Mayfield, how can I help you?" April identified herself and quickly explained her situation to him, then asked for his help in explaining why his firm made a payment each year for a vehicle registration in her county.

The lawyer said, "Well, it does not seem that this would break any attorney/client trust so give me a second and I will look this up for you." Again the seconds waiting seemed like an eternity, but April waited patiently. A quick thought about Amanda flashed in her head and she hoped that she was still alive. Hopefully she would be able to set her free very soon. The attorney's voice came back on the line and he said, "Detective Sanchez?" She said, "Yes." He cleared his throat and said, "What this is about concerns a trust. It was set up years ago by a client named Albert Feller from Little Rock. He was dying of cancer at the time and wanted to leave his home and money to his only remaining family."

April hurried him and said, "Go on please." He said, "He had a will drawn up by our firm, then set up a trust fund to pay his two nephews on a monthly basis. He also left them a house, a van, and a ten thousand dollar life insurance policy. They were not able to collect on it because he had not named them as the beneficiaries. His wife was his beneficiary, but she had passed before him and he had never made the change."

April said, "Is there names and address listed for the nephews?" He said, "Let's see, yes. One, the oldest, is Will Feller. He was named as the executor on the will. The younger nephew is named Phil Darnell. I have two addresses listed here but don't know why, hold on." Again she waited as she wrote the names down, then he came back on the line again and said, "Apparently the funds ran out of the trust fund except for four hundred dollars. We had to contact the two nephews to let them know that and the younger one, the one named Darnell, instructed us just to use the rest to continue paying for the vehicle registration. We had a difficult time getting ahold of him at first but we eventually did. He informed us that Will Feller was not living anymore, then he gave us a different address to mail information to in order to get a power of attorney made for him."

April copied that down next, then said, "Why do the brothers have different names?" The attorney said, "Mr. Albert Feller told us that they were actually step brothers. Apparently their father remarried and the younger son kept his own name. His uncle called him Bear, said it was what he went by." April smiled into the phone now that the mystery had been cleared up, then she said, "So the van they received belonged to their uncle, and that was why the registration was kept in his name correct?"

He said, "That is correct, and, by the way, the last payment we made for the registration was the final one. All of the funds are now depleted." She said, "I don't think he will be needing it anymore." She understood clearly now, thanked him and asked him to forward copies of what he had just revealed to her attention.

April called Sheriff Thomas and explained what she had just learned to him, then said, "We have two addresses now, and I bet that he still lives at the new one that we have now. I need to get out there now and see if I can find Amanda Webb." Sheriff Thomas said, "I will arrange for back-up for you. Make sure that you contact Special Agent Foster before you go, and be careful." April hung up then called Sharon immediately, quickly told her everything that she had learned, then Sharon said, "We're on our way. I'll pull up the address and see if we can get a map and a layout of the property before I leave."

April felt the adrenaline flowing through her as she prepared to leave. She had a name and address now, and she felt that this had to be it. She wanted desperately to find Amanda. She ran to her car and called Sharon. Sharon said, "We're on the road, be there in less than ten minutes. I was able to get a map, and get this, the address is on the same property that we went to initially where we found the abandoned house. One of my agents had a thought that makes sense. He said that the house was probably the one that belonged to the father. The other address is on the same property, but a couple of miles further south. The map shows a large creek running through it."

April said, "And that's how he is able to fish for a living, right on his land. See you shortly." Minutes later two FBI cars pulled up next to her car and Sharon got out and made a circle in the air with her index finger for everyone to gather around. She spread the map on April's hood, then they began to make a plan to approach the home. In less than two minutes they pulled out of the parking lot, and six other deputies followed behind. The sirens and light bars were on as they sped down Route 298, and April hoped that they would not be too late.

Chapter 17

He woke up and felt dizzy for a moment, then slowly got up, using the small table to balance himself. A second later he took a quick look around and saw that he was trapped in the room again. He cussed loudly as he rushed the door, then began kicking at the lock. This time the door gave much faster, and it popped open as the wood around the lock splintered. He rushed out and ran into his bedroom, then yelled as he saw that his backpack was missing. He opened the small nightstand drawer and grabbed his key for the van and rushed outside.

He could not find Amanda anywhere, so he climbed into the van, started it, then pulled away. Immediately he knew that he had a problem. The front was flat. He pounded the steering wheel and cursed loudly, then he opened the door and looked at the tire. It had been blown out, and he realized that Amanda had to have shot it. He knew that she had his gun and backpack with her, but he had to get to her and find her or she would bring the cops to him. He saw the footsteps in the dirt road and saw that she took to the road again, so he took off running after her as fast as he could.

For the first time in days he felt fear, but he knew that he could resolve his problem once he found her. Even though she had his gun he knew that she would be afraid to use it on him, so he knew that he was going to be able to grab her. This time he would take her on the spot then strangle the life out of her. He was breathing hard already as he ran, and he knew that once he made it around the bend he would be able to spot her on the long, dirt road. His mind was filled with rage as he ran, and all that he could think of was making her pay for what she had done.

Amanda had slowed down, then finally began to walk at a steady pace. She stopped for a moment to grab one of the juice drinks out of the backpack. She looked behind her and did not see him coming, then she decided to just set a steady pace walking fast to save her energy and keep going. This dirt road had to go somewhere she thought, besides, she had the loaded gun with her and she knew that there was no way she was ever going to let him take her back. She also knew that if he caught her he would rape and kill her. Out here no one would ever find her body.

As she walked on she began thinking about her family again, and her spirits climbed as she now had hope that she would be with them again. She looked back as she walked because she knew that he was coming after her, but she was determined to make it out of this place somehow.

He made the bend and saw her far ahead. She was walking down the middle of the dirt road as if she was out on a hike. He was winded and tired and had to slow down to a trot, but he ran along the side of the road to use the trees and brush for cover. Hopefully she wouldn't see him until he was close. Once he got ahold of her she was going to be sorry that she had put him in this situation. He was going to take her into the brush, rape her, then leave her to rot there after he drained the life out of her. He wished that he had thought to bring something to use as a weapon, so he started looking on the side of the road for a large branch or rock to use as he ran slowly.
Although his side hurt and his leg muscles began to burn, he was not about to quit. If she got out on the paved road and some car came by he was going to really be in trouble. He let out a low growl and felt the anger rising in him, and he increased his pace without realizing it.

The newly formed task force made excellent time down Route 298, and already familiar with the dirt road's location, April, whose car was in the lead, slowed to make the turn. She glanced back in her rearview mirror and saw the other vehicles following close behind. There was a bend on the road ahead and, if she remembered correctly, the house she and Sharon had first gone to was about two or so miles past that first bend.

Amanda kept going. She had drained the juice bottle and was glad that she had thought to bring them. It was hot out and the sun was blaring down on her, covering her with sweat. Her body ached from the beating she had been given, and the straps from the backpack hurt her shoulders, but she was not going to leave it behind. She knew that the money inside of it belonged to the people he had murdered, and she was going to give it to the police as evidence. She could not wait to see the police and to see her family.

Suddenly she heard sounds coming from far ahead and began to stare as she began to increase her pace. The faster she went, the louder the sounds she heard, then she realized that what she was hearing were sirens. The police, that had to be the police! She felt excited now and let out a small cry as she now began to run. A few moments later she saw the flashing light of a car as it made it around a bend on the road, then she saw that there were a lot of police cars coming. She yelled out, "Yes! I'm here!"

She turned around now and saw him. He was running after her, but she watched as he suddenly stopped and put both hands on his knees as he bent at the waist. She looked back at the police, then back at him again, and now she watched him turn around and begin to run back. She didn't care anymore, she wanted desperately to get to the police, so she began to waive her arms in the air as she ran.

Suddenly April saw someone running down the middle of the dirt road and slowed down to get a better look. She was about a hundred yards away now, and she could see that it was a woman running and waiving her arms in the air. She was in trouble, and April sped up again. As she drew close she saw the woman clearly now and yelled out, "It's her, its Amanda!" She realized that she was alone in the car and came to a stop about twenty yards before her and got out. She looked at Amanda then saw that she was carrying a pistol in her hands, so she put her arms out and yelled for her to stop.

It took a moment for the elated Amanda to comprehend her signal, but she stopped running and dropped her arms to her side. April yelled out, "It's OK Amanda, drop the gun on the ground." Amanda looked at her quizzically for a moment, then she realized that she had been waiving a gun wildly at the police. She gasped and stepped back as she flung the pistol to the ground, then she broke down, fell to her knees, and began to cry. Her shoulders heaved as she wailed loudly finally knowing that she was free.

April ran to her as Sharon and two of her agents ran a few steps behind her. One of the agents ran towards the pistol and stood over it as Sharon and April knelt down beside the young woman. Sharon said, "It's her! It's Amanda! Unbelievable!" Amanda looked up as she removed her hands from her face, then she hugged the two women as she cried. They both comforted her for a few moments, reassuring her that she was safe now. Amanda nodded because she understood that, but she was overwhelmed with emotions. It took another few moments for her to stand, then she pointed down the road and said, "He was running after me. I saw him. He stopped then turned and started running back the other way."

April and Sharon looked at each other, then Sharon said, "I'll stay here with her and call for an ambulance. Go after him."

Amanda put her hand up and said, "Wait. I have his backpack. It had that gun in it, and there's money and other stuff in it." She took it off and handed it to Sharon, then Sharon opened it and showed the cash to April. April shook her head then said, "Amanda, did he have a gun on him?" Amanda said, "I, I don't think so, but I couldn't tell for sure. I hit him over the head and escaped. I used his gun to shoot a tire out on his van, then I ran away." The two law enforcement officers looked at each other in amazement, then April said, "Was it a white van?" Amanda nodded, then said, "Yes, and it smelled like fish."

April ran back to her car and told everyone that the kidnapper was on foot. They all ran back to their cars and began to follow April as she sped down the dirt road, throwing clouds of dust everywhere. Sharon put her arm around Amanda and smiled at her, then she said, "Come on Amanda, let's go to my car. My name is Sharon Foster, and I'm with the FBI. Amanda smiled at her and followed her to the car. She knew that, somehow she had made it, then she thanked God for His help and took a seat in the air conditioning.

He was really scared now. His chest hurt and his legs felt like rubber, but he knew that if he stopped he was going to be caught. Sweat ran down his face and his throat felt like it was on fire, but he could not stop now. He heard the sirens, then the second he saw a flashing blue light he turned and started running as fast as he could. He knew that in a matter of minutes the police would come after him. That bitch Amanda would tell them that he had been following her. He looked ahead and only saw more dirt road, and the bend of the road was still a good ways ahead. He knew that there was no way he was going to be able to make it back home, and that he had to get off the road now or he was going to get caught.

He stopped and turned but did not see them coming yet, and he did not hear the sirens either, but they could have turned them off. He was out of breath and breathing heavily, but he took a look at the brush on the side of the road and started for it. Since he lived out here he was familiar with the area, and he knew that he could get away and hide somewhere, but he was tired and thirsty, and the cops would be fresh. He started making wailing sounds as he trudged through the brush. Branches hit him in the face and arms as he panicked and ran through them instead of around them. He had to find a place to hide and he needed water real bad, so he kept going as fast as he was able to, running in a panic mode through the brush.

April drove fast as she looked for him, making all the way to the bend of the road and still did not see him. If he was running after Amanda and she had seen him, that meant that he could not have been too far behind. She had driven past him. He had to have turned off the dirt road somewhere, so she told her deputies to start looking for his tracks as they circled back. A half mile down the road they spotted his footprints as they headed into the brush and stopped.

April called Sheriff Thomas and asked for the helicopter to come out and explained that the killer had gone into the woods. He told her he would send more people and dogs to use to track him down, and she told him that she and her deputies were going to pursue now. She told everyone to keep an eye out for his footprints as she stepped into the brush and began to give chase. She knew that he had been on foot and had to tire soon, and that she and her deputies would gain the advantage then, but she understood that in these heavy woods he could easily hide from them also.

Special Agent Foster had called for an ambulance, then she called her office and asked a fellow agent to contact Amanda's family and explain to them that she was alive and well but was going to be taken to the local hospital to be checked out. She looked at Amanda and saw her smiling for the first time, then she patted her on her leg and said, "Soon you'll see your mom and dad Amanda." Amanda nodded and tears began to form in her eyes, but they were tears of joy.

They heard the siren before they saw the paramedics arrive. Amanda was transferred to the ambulance and Sharon smiled at her and said, "I will need to speak with you about what happened, but I want you to let the doctors check you out. Your family will meet you at the hospital. Please do not speak with anyone about what took place until I speak with you OK?" Amanda nodded, then said, "Thank you for coming after me." Sharon shook her head at her and said, "Well, you are welcome, but it looked to me that you were quite capable of getting away from that monster on your own. What you did took a lot of courage, and I am very proud of you." Sharon watched the ambulance drive away then she got on her radio and called April. Once she found out that they were in the brush she rushed to the spot where they went in to help them in the search.

They had a new agenda now, and that was to find the killer and bring him to justice. She hoped that he had not raped the young Amanda, but if she discovered that he had she was going to make him pay dearly.

Chapter 18

He was down to a walk now. His whole body hurt. His leg muscles ached and he was sucking in air, having to stop several times just so that he would not pass out. He leaned on his knees and breathed heavily as he looked back. He knew that he had a good head start on the police, and out here in the thick woods it was going to be almost impossible to find him, but he also knew that they would bring dogs to track him soon enough and more people too.

He kept going slowly, thinking about his need for finding water. He had to find some water or he was going to die out here. He finally stopped to rest and to think, partly because he had no choice, since he was tired and winded and had to stop. Now that he calmed down some he felt like he was more in control of his situation than he had at first. He was the one familiar with this area, not them. He just had to find water so that he could increase his pace and get away. Covered in sweat, he knew then that he had to make it water real soon. He knew the creeks in the area better than anyone else, and once he made it to the water he would circle back and find his boat.

If he could make it to the river he would lose them for certain, so he stood straight, took several breaths and let them out slowly, then began to walk again. This time he changed direction and began heading south. There would be water in that direction, and that also meant freedom.

April and her team had a difficult time following his tracks. At times they would find a print in the sugar sand or dirt, then they would lose it again only to find it heading in another direction. She knew that he had to be tired, and she wished that she could run after him and just catch him, but it was difficult to tell what direction he was headed in. At least he wasn't going to be able to get back to his home again.

She wished that she knew more about Bear Darnell than she

knew, but she had to just keep trying to locate his tracks for now. Her team was on high alert as they walked through the thick brush and under the canopy of large trees. Every now and then someone would call out that they spotted a track, then everyone would head towards it. She really wanted to find this guy and lock him up before he hurt or killed anyone else. She felt sweat running down her face now as she hurried through the woods, but she kept looking ahead for signs of the escaped killer.

As more deputies arrived on the scene, Sharon dispatched some of them to the address she had for Darnell. She had entered the woods and began to try to track April, but she found out real quick that she was not able to. She called her and told her that she was going to investigate Darnell's house, and that she now heard the helicopter arriving. She turned back and joined the other deputies as they drove ahead to spot Darnell's house.

At first Sharon was not surprised to see the location of Darnell's house, but once they all entered and found the room he had turned into a prison and saw the chains attached to the wall, they were all disgusted. She shook her head and wondered about what abuse and torture Amanda must have gone through at the hands of that monster. She had not asked her if he had raped her because her primary concern was to get her to the hospital. She looked malnourished and she had seen the red welts on her body and it had angered her, and after seeing the condition of the home now she understood more about her captor. She called the crime scene unit to the home and had them go through it thoroughly, gathering DNA evidence, finger prints, and whatever other evidence they could use to convict him.

She saw the van and the tire that Amanda had shot out and smiled, knowing that her quick thinking under stress had most likely helped save her life. She hoped that her team members hunting that scumbag would be successful and find him. A man like that was dangerous to anyone he encountered, and he would show no empathy to those he crossed paths with.

Bear, who had been given that nickname by his uncle when he was a child, was desperate. He kept going through the woods hoping to spot a familiar area, but he had not been in the thicket of the forest before. Even when he hunted out here he had certain spots that he would go to and all of them were close to the river or a creek. He knew that he was headed in the right direction, so he kept his pace up. He had to, or he would die out there.

April was in the lead and was having trouble finding his footprints. She stopped and turned, then said, "Is there anyone here that can do a better job at finding his tracks? I'm trying but it's not my cup of tea." One of her deputies named Sam Freemont stepped forward and said, "Let me try Detective Sanchez. I hunted all of my life and my dad taught me to track animals. Maybe I'll have some luck." He took the lead and within five minutes found a set of tracks and said, "He stopped here, then it looks like he changed directions, look." He pointed to a spot on the ground where his boots had made deeper indentations, then he said, "It looks to me like he stopped here. Maybe he was worn out and had to, but he decided for some reason to go that way." He pointed south, then April said, "He knows the area better than we do, and my bet is that he's heading to water, come on."

She called the helicopter and tried to steer them in a southerly direction as she and her team began their search in that direction. She figured that if he made it to the river he would have a greater advantage, so she increased her pace as she followed Deputy Freemont.

Amanda arrived at the hospital, then she was examined by two doctors right away. They bombarded her with a bunch of questions as they attached inter-veinous solutions to her, and she found herself growing tired quickly. Before she realized it she closed her eyes and fell asleep, finally resting peacefully with the knowledge that she was safe now and would be seeing her family real soon.

Bear stopped again. He was real tired, achy, and covered with sweat. His throat felt like it was on fire, and licking his dry lips did nothing to make him feel any better. The heat was too much to bear but he knew that if he kept going he would find a creek. He trudged on through the thick woods and finally he saw what looked like a clearing ahead. With hope in his heart now he found new energy to make a burst towards it, then he let out a cry of joy when he saw the water. He had made it! Up ahead was part of one of the many creeks that fed into the Ouachita River, and it meant salvation.

He ran up to the water then fell at the banks lapping water into his mouth with both hands. He sighed with relief as he splashed the water all over his head and arms, then he stood and walked into it. The water felt great as he dunked his whole body into it, and he let out another sound of pure joy as he realized that he had just struck gold. A moment later reality set in and he turned to look behind him. He knew that the police were behind him and would find him soon, so he turned and looked at the creek. He was not familiar with this one, and he had to stop a moment to think of which direction to go.

He knew that he had gone south, and now he needed to go right and head east. A few miles ahead would be his small dock, and there he would find his boat. If he found it he could get away from this area and get to safety, so he got out of the water and began walking along the creek, heading east.

He started thinking about Amanda as he walked, and he felt the anger rising once again. She had fooled him and had managed to escape, and now he had lost his home, his van, and his hard earned money. He had no weapons to defend himself with either, and it was all her fault. For now his first priority was to escape, then he would decide if he was going to seek revenge on her later. He felt fear now as he walked along and constantly looked in all directions for any signs of the police.

April's team had found a set of tracks and saw a clearing

ahead. Deputy Freemont saw the water first and called everyone up to him. As soon as they arrived at the water's edge they all saw his tracks clearly. April said, "Crap, he made it to water. He's going to try to use the river to escape. Can you continue tracking him Sam?" Sam Freemont smiled at her and said, "Since he's more concerned about getting away in a hurry and he's not trying to cover his tracks, then yeah, I can track him. Come on!"

They filed single file behind him and increased their pace as he seemed to be able to track quite easily. April called her chopper and told them about the creek and heard it minutes later before it flew over their heads heading east. She hoped that they would be able to spot him but she knew that he was traveling through the edge of the forest under the canopy of the trees. Bear had to be close, but he also had the advantage of knowing where he was headed and all that they could do was to follow.

Her radio chirped and she took a call from fellow Deputy Ana Bell. She informed April that she had a team of dogs and several deputies and asked her where to go. April knew that she was headed east but she had no idea where she would be on a map. She did her best to let Ana know an approximate location, telling her to find a creek and follow it west. She had no idea how far away they were, so all that she could do was to hope that they could intersect Bear Darnell up ahead of her own team.

She took a call from Special Agent Foster and learned about what she had found in his home. The deputies with her all heard about the chains and the sound proofed room and all wanted to find him even more. Deputy Freemont gave another call that he had fresh tracks again, and they increased their pace again. She wondered how far ahead he was as she followed her deputy, and hoped that they would be able to spot him soon. If they were not able to find him during the daylight hours he would be able to slip away.

Bear was feeling much better now. He saw a bend in the creek ahead and it looked familiar. He started running now hoping that he would recognize the area, then as he reached the bend he said, "Yeah!" He had been here before. This meant that his dock was less than a half mile away. He looked behind him and did not see any of the cops he knew were following, and started running at a slow, but steady pace. The water had done his body wonders by giving him a burst of energy. If he made it to his boat he knew that he had bottle water and food in it that he always kept for when he would go out fishing.

Even more important than that was the fact that he would navigate his way out of the area and head to a spot he alone knew about. One of the many hundreds of small coves that intertwined throughout the creek, it was desolate and there would be no way he would be spotted there, from the water or the air. Suddenly he heard a helicopter approaching and he gasped. He looked up and saw that he was still under the cover of the tree canopy, but up ahead the woods thinned out and he would be out in the open.

He was worried now because he knew that he could not stay under cover of the forest and wait for the chopper to leave the area. If he stopped, the cops following him would catch up, but if he made a run for it and get out in the open area the helicopter was sure to spot him. He turned around again as his eyes widened with fear. Still no sign of anyone behind him, he looked ahead and tried to make a decision. The helicopter kept circling the air above him as they too saw the clearing. They knew that he had to be hiding where he was even though they could not see him, and they also knew that he would have to get into the clearing if he wanted to leave the area. He cried out with fear, not knowing what to do next.

Chapter 19

The crime scene unit had found a treasure of evidence in Darnell's home and were able to gather DNA evidence to use to convict him of the murders. Special Agent Foster kept in contact with April and knew that they were getting closer to finding him. April learned about the clearing ahead and knew that he had not crossed over it yet. Her helicopter was hovering in the area trying to spot him, and now Deputy Ana Bell called to let her know that they had found a dock with a boat not far from the back of Darnell's home.

April thought a moment, then she called out that the boat had to be Bear Darnell's boat, and that he was headed for it. She knew that she was close now, and everyone was on high alert anticipating seeing him real soon. Deputy Bell posted two deputies at the dock and began heading in a westerly direction with her dogs and four other deputies, and April knew that now Bear Darnell was trapped. It was just a matter of time now before they flushed him out, so she came up with an idea to make him think that he was going to able to escape.

Darnell heard the helicopter leaving the area and breathed a sigh of relief. With it out of the way he now had a clear path to reach his boat. He took one last look behind him then he bolted from under the tree canopy. He made the clearing and ran as fast as he could even though his leg muscles ached and burned. He was sucking in air as he ran, staying close to the edge of the creek because the brush there was minimal. He felt great because he knew that he was going to get to his boat in minutes.

April called Deputy Bell and advised her of her plan, then she and her team spread out and increased their pace as they followed along the edge of the creek. She was hoping to lure him out by making him think that the helicopter had left the area for good. She had Deputy Bell and her team waiting ahead of her with their dogs, and with her own team close behind him, she felt that it was only a matter of minutes before they reached him.

Bear Darnell finally saw the clearing come to a spot where a large boulder stuck out into the creek. Just on the other side of it was the dock where his boat was located, and it was about a hundred yards away. He stopped running then and turned to look behind him. He did not see anyone yet but he knew that by now the police had to have raided his house. He believed that they would find his spare boat keys there and learn that he had a boat, then they would come to search for it.

Because his dock was not too far from his house he believed that they would be able to follow the trail and find it easily, so he decided to do something smart and head into the water. Once in the creek he could easily make the swim from the other side of the bank and be able to see if the cops were waiting for him there at his dock. If he ran straight ahead he may run into their waiting arms, so he waded into the water and swam across the creek, then he began to swim slowly towards his dock. If the police were there waiting, he would see them and turn around, then he would cross to the other side of the creek and wait for them to leave before he would attempt to take his boat.

He swam slowly, doing a breast stroke, his head the only visible part in the water. He knew that the police would be looking on land for his approach, not in the water itself. He slowed as he passed by the large boulder, then he peered straight ahead and saw two deputies standing on his boat dock. One of them had a foot on his boat as they both looked towards the same direction he would have come from. They knew that he was headed their way.

He felt glad that he had made the decision to swim in instead of being foolish to keep running or walking. He would have fallen right into their hands. But he had out smarted them. He smiled inwardly with pride as he waded in the water, then he began to swim back slowly so as not to cause any ripples in the water. He made it around the boulder and swam towards the shore line to find a good hiding spot in case the helicopter came back. He could not hear it now, so he felt safe. In thirty seconds he would be looking for a good tree nearby to hide under while he waited for the cops to leave.

April and her team made it out of the clearing now and saw the large boulder ahead. Deputy Freemont found fresh tracks and stopped, calling his team to him. He pointed to them as he placed his index finger to his lips to let everyone know to be silent. He lowered his voice to a whisper and said, "He stopped here and went into the water. He probably wanted to swim to his dock to see if we had people on it waiting there for him." April smiled and patted him on the shoulder as she said, "Great job Sam. Once he sees the deputies on the dock he's going to swim back and cross over just like we thought. Deputy Bell will be waiting for him."

They all continued on slowly until they saw the dock ahead and stopped. They searched the water but did not see him in it, and they all knew that he had made it across and smiled.

Deputy Ana Bell was the one that had come up with the idea to split her team up. She took one deputy with her and crossed the creek, making the short swim to the other side, then they waited in the brush for him to appear. She watched him coming and radioed April, then she and the other deputy slid back into the brush as they watched him enter the water. They wanted to wait for him to cross over and grab him at that moment because he would never be expecting it and have his guard down.

She was not able to see if he had a weapon on him, but she saw his hands were not holding one because he used them to swim the breast stroke. She and her other deputy laid flat as he passed by, then watched him swim ahead and stop. They knew that at that moment he had made their two men on the boat dock, then they watched him slowly make his way back as they laid flat once again.

Bear was almost to the bank and swam into one of his trot

lines. He stopped a moment and thought that this felt like he was a fish waiting to be caught unaware by the bait on the trot line. He wondered if he was swimming into a trap and listened. A quick turn as he glanced and he did not see any signs of the police, but something told him that he had to be careful. He felt fear once again as he contemplated what his next move was. Once the feeling of dread passed him, he decided that he was right in thinking that he had to get to the other bank and hide out there til dark.

He made a few more strokes, stood in the water, then walked out and headed into the brush. He kept low so that he would not be spotted, then he saw a row of scrub oak trees ahead and headed for them. They were large enough to provide cover from both above and from the side, and he felt that he had made the right decision. He slid into them and leaned on one of the small trees as his breathing began to return to normal. He had made it. All that he had to do now was to wait until dark. By then the cops would have figured that he had escaped them and leave the dock. All he would need to do then was to swim to the boat and use his trolling motor to leave the area, then he would start his Yamaha outboard and take off. He would not need to use his running lights on board because he knew the water like the back of his own hand.

He started to relax for the first time since he had first entered the woods, and he closed his eyes as he laid back on the tree. That was the moment that he heard, "Don't move or we shoot! Bear Darnell you are under arrest." Darnell jumped and gasped as his eyes opened, then he saw a pistol pointed at his face and heard a woman's voice from his left. A male deputy was standing in front of him as another deputy, a woman, came from his side. He yelled, "No!" as he watched the female officer grab him and turn him on his side, then he felt the handcuffs going on his wrists. They were talking to him but he could not make out what they were saying because he started wailing. To his surprise, tears began to flow from his eyes as he was turned sideways, then he felt himself being searched. He was turned the opposite way, then searched again, then a moment later the male deputy picked him up off the ground and turned him to face them.

He looked at both of their faces in shock as he wondered how they had managed to sneak up on him. He had not seen them and he had been careful to look in every direction. Now he watched as the female deputy called in on her radio, and he heard her tell everyone that they had him in custody. He heard their shouts of joy over the radio just then, and he hung his head in shame as the male deputy shoved him forward to get moving. Now he heard them begin to read him his rights, then they stopped him to ask if he understood them. He nodded, but they the woman deputy said, "Say it out loud, do you understand your rights?" He said, "Yeah, got it."

They led him out and into the water as they both held his arms to keep his head afloat. Once they reached the other side of the bank a bunch of deputies were there waiting. They helped them all out of the water, then headed for his doc where two more deputies waited. One was holding the key to his boat in his hand. He smiled at him and said, "You didn't think that we would just go and leave you the key did you? We found where you hid it and had it in our hands." He laughed and other deputies joined in as a woman approached him.

He recognized her from the television, and knew that she was Detective Sanchez, the one that the Sheriff had announced as heading the investigation. She had a big smile on her face as she said, "Even though you were read your rights I am going to repeat them again while we record it on our body cameras." She read his rights and had him acknowledge that he understood them, then she said, Phil Darnell, also known as Bear, you are under arrest for kidnapping Amanda Webb, and the murder of Dolores Richards, and Karen and Robin Potter, with more charges to be charged to you later."

He was led back to his home and saw more officers and police dogs standing waiting for him to pass by. He glanced towards his house as he was led past it where another woman waited by a car. She too was smiling when they brought him to a stop in front of her, then she said, "Bear, I am Special Agent Sharon Foster of the FBI. You are coming with me, and we are going to have us a little chat." He was placed in the back of a police car, then he watched the FBI woman hug Detective Sanchez and the woman deputy that had arrested him. They all turned and looked at him now and he turned his face away.

He closed his eyes a moment and wondered how he had come to this point. If it had not been for that moment when he first saw Amanda broken down by the side of the road, he would still be carrying on with his normal lifestyle. He would gladly trade that now for what he was about to go through. As the patrol car he was in pulled away from his home he took one last look at it knowing that he would never see it again. More tears flowed from his eyes as his shoulder started to heave slowly.

Chapter 20

Amanda had reunited with her family and was released from the hospital. They were saddened when they saw her condition at first, but happy to learn that she had not been raped. Both April and Sharon had interviewed her and got the whole story, then the media interviewed her and her family. While they were being interviewed Amanda had not yet learned that her captor had been captured, and the news that they would hear later would send chills through her and her family.

The deputy escorting Bear back to the prison to be booked in made the turn on Route 298 and began heading east. He glanced in the rearview mirror and saw that the prisoner had his dead down. He could not feel sorry for him though because he knew that this man had not shown any compassion to those whose life he had taken. He built up speed until he was cruising at 60 mph., then he saw the turn ahead. Instead of slowing down to take it at a safer speed, he glanced back at the rearview mirror again and slightly smiled. Maybe a little fun wouldn't hurt. So what if the prisoner was flung against the other window just because he had a bit of fun. He could always explain that he was trying to get out of the car and did not see the bend in the road coming.

The deputy stepped on the accelerator just before entering the bend in the road, then he gripped the steering wheel ready to take the turn at a high speed. Just as he made the bend a deer was crossing the road at that moment, and the shock of seeing it prevented the deputy from reacting a split second later. At the last second he swung the steering wheel hard left to avoid hitting the animal, but at that rate of speed he began to fishtail, then the car turned over and began to roll off the road.

Bear had his hands in handcuffs but had not had the seatbelt attached, so he felt himself flying upwards as his head hit the ceiling of the car. Both men were yelling as the vehicle rolled out of control, and Bear was tumbling around in the back seat as the car, traveling at a high rate of speed came as it came into contact with a tree and stopped suddenly. Bear hit the back of the front seat, the cage in the back kept him confined to a small space during the roll over. Just as quick as the accident occurred, there was now dead silence as the patrol car bent around the tree.

Bear slowly came to and he looked around him. He did not hear a sound as he began to groan in pain. He was lying face down on the back floor and had no idea what had happened. He slowly got into the back seat as he groaned, then found he could not sit up because the roof had caved in. It was then that he was able to see that the cage holding him in the back had been mangled. He saw the body of the deputy still in the seat, but from his angle it looked like the front and top of his head had been smashed. Bear called out to him to see if he could get his handcuffs off, afraid that the car would catch fire any second. He yelled several times but got no response, then he saw the opening in the cage and began to move.

It took him almost ten minutes to make it to the front seat and maneuver his body to where he could reach the deputy's pocket. Slowly he slid his hand in and felt around. Nothing. He was hurting but he had to get out of the car before it caught fire, so he pulled the dead deputy back as far as he could and searched his top shirt pocket. He let out a shout of joy when his fingers felt the small handcuff key, then he grabbed it gently, positioned it in his hand, and pulled away. Another few moments later he felt the cuffs release, then he felt instant relief. He was free.

The next few minutes were exhausting as Bear tried his best to find a way out of the crushed vehicle. He grunted as he kicked, but the only door not crushed in would not open. Out of breath now he had to pause as he began to feel panic, then he eyed the pistol that was still on the dead deputy's holster. He grabbed it and shot out the rear window, then slid out of it.

He tried to stand up but fell to the ground, then he slowly

crawled away from the vehicle and laid on the ground until he caught his breath. Not feeling dizzy anymore, he stood slowly, then felt that he could walk. One last look at the wreckage, then he looked at the road ahead and began to walk to it. He could not believe that he was alive and free, and even better than that he now had a gun. He knew that the rest of the cops would be coming by soon, so he had to get away from there as fast as possible. He looked down the road and did not see anyone, but when he looked in the direction where they were originally heading he saw a car approaching.

Thinking quickly, he stuck the pistol in the small of his back and began to waive his hands in the air. Moments later the car slowed as it got close, then he pointed back to the scene of the accident as it came to a complete stop. The couple in the car both looked and saw the mangled patrol car, then both turned to look at him. The man opened his window and said, "My God! Are you alright sir?" Bear managed to show him a weak smile as he pulled the pistol from his back, then he said, "I am now."

The first deputy that had departed from the scene went by the area of the wreck just five minutes later. He was so focused on the road ahead that he did not see the accident on his left. The patrol car had rolled quite a ways off the road and on the road itself there were no indications that anything had happened at all. He continued going on Route 298 without ever seeing it, but the other two deputies traveling minutes behind him both saw it and immediately called it in. The first deputy could not believe what he just heard as he turned to head back to offer assistance. Moments after arriving at the scene of the accident Detective Sanchez received a call that totally caught her by surprise.

She heard the deputy on the radio describing the scene of the accident, then calling for an ambulance. Moments later, before she had a chance to speak with her deputy, she heard the horrible news that the deputy escorting the prisoner was not breathing. Before all of that had a chance to register in her brain the real shock came when she heard the excitement in her deputy's voice as he now announced that there was no sign of the prisoner, and that the deputy's pistol was missing. April could not believe what she was hearing as she sped to the scene herself.

Even though she was alone in her car she said aloud, "Dear God no!" She called her deputy and had him do a thorough search around the area to make sure that the pistol had not somehow dislodged itself and ended up flying away during the course of the crash. She already knew that it was not really possible, but she was hopeful that it would be found. To have her prisoner escape was bad enough, but to know that he was now armed was too much to take in. Still not believing that something like this had just happened, she saw the other patrol cars around the scene of the accident and pulled in behind them.

After taking a quick look around and not seeing any signs of the prisoner, she ran back to her car and called it in, letting her dispatcher know that he was now armed. April leaned back on her car door stunned as she looked at the wreckage. She felt horrible for the young officer that had lost his life, and at the same time she felt anger that Bear Darnell had escaped. He had not even tried to offer assistance to her deputy. He may have been alive and pulling him out of the wreck and administering CPR may have saved his life. But Bear Darnell was not that type of person. Bear Darnell was a murderer and a kidnapper, and now he was loose once again. She slammed the door with her hand and cussed as she looked down the highway. There was no way to know which direction he took, and even though some of her deputies had headed out in both directions, April believed that a car had come by and he had stopped it, and by now he was on his way to who knows where.

She hit the door again several times and cursed some more before she heard the siren from the approaching ambulance. She called Sheriff Thomas to let him know what had taken place there as she headed back to the station. She hoped that her people would find him along the road, but she knew better than to even think that was possible.

The couple, in their mid-twenties, were both horrified as their car headed east on the highway. The woman was crying as her husband drove, then she heard the large man in the back seat telling her to keep quiet or he would shoot her. Her husband pleaded with him but the man put the gun to the back of his wife's head and told him to keep quiet or he would see his wife's brains splattered all over the dash. He begged him not to hurt her, then Bear said, "Shut up and stay focused on the road. Drive the speed limit and don't try anything stupid or I will kill her immediately."

The man asked where he was going, then Bear said, "I want you to take me out of the area. Head north on Route 7 and keep going." The couple, traveling east on Route 298, were both scared and held hands as they headed east. A mile later they saw the sign that Route 7 was two miles ahead, then Bear told him to take it north again, reminding him that he had his gun on the wife and would not hesitate to use it if he did anything but what he was told. The husband reassured him that he was obeying him and asked for him not to hurt her again, then Bear said, "I told you to keep quiet. Say one more thing to me, either of you, and I blow her brains out. Now drive!"

The woman cried again as her husband squeezed her hand to try reassuring her, and Bear slid down as they heard the sound of a siren approaching. Just as they made the turn onto Route 7 to head north, an ambulance made the turn onto the road they had just been on. The couple both wandered what their captor had done, both fearing for their lives even more now. Bear sat up again and looked at the road ahead. There was a lot more traffic on this road, so he made sure that no police cars were nearby and said, "I want you to just keep going north. Up ahead about 35 or 40 miles is a sign for Nimrod Dam. You're gonna take that road to the left. I can't remember the number, but it's the only left turn. You are looking for a sign for Nimrod Lake. Keep going on that road once you make the turn."

He had been to the large lake a few times to fish and knew that only the locals ever visited it. It was a large lake and the police would never suspect that he was headed there. He needed time to think so that he would not make a wrong move. He had a car now, two hostages, and a gun. He felt real thirsty and hungry then and asked if they had anything to eat or drink. They told him no, so he ordered the husband to slow up at the intersection of Forest Service road ahead and pull into the convenience store.

Less than a mile later they saw the intersection and slowed, then the car pulled into the small convenience store and Bear told him to park on the side. He said, "I want you to listen to me very carefully now. I want the wifey here to go inside and buy me several bottles of water, candy bars and potato chips, then grab me pizza or a hot dog, whatever they have that's hot. I will have the gun on your husband's head. If you want to see him alive again you just go in, buy the stuff, then leave. Try to warn anyone or any other little trick and a cop comes along, I will kill you both and take the car. The only way you both are going to live is if you do exactly what I tell you. Wipe your face and get those tears cleaned up and do not blow this or hubby here will go straight to hell, now get going and hurry."

The woman looked at her husband and he tried to smile at her, then he gave her cash and said, "We can do this babe. Just do what he says. Once we take him to where he wants to go he'll let us go. Go on now." Bear heard him and said, "Remember, hubby dies if you screw up." The wife opened the door and walked into the store as Bear looked around. He had avoided the camera at the gasoline pump and was not going to risk going in the store, so he looked around at the cars going by on the road. He decided to calm the man down and make sure that he would feel he and his wife were going to be OK once he released them, so he lowered his voice to make it sound sincere and said, "Look, I'm desperate to get away from here. Like you told your wife, once I get out of the area I will take your car. I'll have to take you two someplace where you can't get to a phone so quick, but if you listen and do as you are told you will save your skins. Now, hand over all the cash you have as well as from her purse."

A few minutes later they were on the way again and Bear could tell that the man was not so rattled. He was eating two slices of pizza and drinking his second bottle of water as they headed north on Route 7. He wanted to get far enough out of the area and he knew that a large lake like Nimrod would be a perfect place to kill the young couple and not have to worry about someone hearing the gun. Although it had been a couple of years since he had been up there, he still remembered that it was a large, remote area that was heavily forested. It was going to be easy to get out of the area once he made it up there.

Chapter 21

Detective Sanchez was joined by FBI Special Agent Foster and Sheriff Thomas as they searched the large county map on the wall at the sub-station. Calls were coming in from patrol units as they covered a large area all the way west to the town of Story, to the east of where Route 298 ended and ran into Route 7. The Sheriff Department chopper was in the air as other law enforcement units from other agencies joined in the search. The only thing that they felt they knew was that Bear Darnell had taken another car. They had no idea if he went east or west on Route 298, then if he had gone north or south on Route 7 if he had gone in that direction.

They felt terrible that one of their own had lost their life, and now had to deal with the media because they had been monitoring their police scanner and learned of the accident. Sheriff Thomas had to issue a statement and warn citizens that an escaped convict was loose. He gave a description of Bear Darnell then ended the news conference without taking any questions. He wanted to focus on finding the escapee, not on answering questions. Without knowing what kind of car Darnell was in and in what direction it was headed, all that they could do was to expand their search and hope that someone would spot him.

Minutes after leaving the convenience store the scenery changed from a rural community to a forested area. A small creek ran alongside the road as they headed north, then they saw the sign for Iron Spring Roadside Park. After going past it, the husband looked at his gas gauge and said, "Uh, mister, we have a little more than a quarter tank of gas left." Darnell cussed and said, "Why did you wait to tell me this now? You think that we're gonna run out and be stranded then you two will be rescued? If you run out of gas you both die, so take it easy and make it last. We have more than enough to get where I'm going, but if you see a gas station ahead pull in."

They traveled over ten more miles before they saw a small station on the opposite side of the road, then Bear told him to pull in and top off. He ducked down as the man got out and filled the tank. The husband was desperate. He did not believe that this guy was going to let them live, but he had told his wife a lie to calm her down and not worry her. He looked at the man sitting behind the glass window and tried to get his attention but could not. This was an old station that only had two pumps and a small building on site large enough to carry a few snack items, and they were the only car at the pump.

He had not paid by credit card, yet the man had turned the pump on once he saw him waive at him. Expecting to see the man come inside to pay, the cashier stood up and began to go outside when he saw the man waive at him then get into the car. The car turned so that he could see the license plate, then it pulled back out on Route 7 slowly as he yelled at them. He ran inside and called 911, then he gave them a plate number, the description of the car, and the fact that he had seen three people in it. He made sure to mention that the third person had suddenly popped his head up once the car made the turn on the road.

The couple fell into a period of silence as the car headed north. The husband began to pray as he glanced at his young wife, then he snuck a look in his rearview mirror and saw the man looking back behind him. He was worried that a police car was close and had not noticed that he had not paid for the gas. He had purposely slowed down once he saw the man coming outside so that he could get a good look at his license plate, and he hoped that he would call the police. He had even used his turn signal to show him that they were headed north, and all that he could do now was to hope the police would come. He slowed a little more than before and was prepared to let their kidnapper know that he did not want to arouse suspicion if he noticed the change in speed. He seemed real preoccupied with looking behind him as they drove and so far had not taken notice.

The call came in to the dispatcher and a unit was dispatched that was in the area, then she contacted the sub-station located north of that location to let them know the car was headed their way. At first she did not catch the fact that the store employee had told her that someone had popped up in the back-seat of the car once it turned, then suddenly she realized what that could mean and called Sheriff Thomas. He asked for all of the details of the call, then he told her to dispatch every available unit to Route 7 north and had her put every unit from the sub-station located on Route 124 by the South Fourche Campground on Route 7 heading south.

Sheriff Thomas knew that there were only five patrol cars working out that area, but he wanted all available units from there on the road to look for the red Toyota that had been described by the service station attendant. Special Agent Foster went with April in her car as they took off and begin to give pursuit, at the same time the department helicopter was re-routed to the area while the Sheriff coordinated a road block up ahead on Route 7. If Darnell was in that car, they had to make sure to stop it as soon as possible. He knew that he had a gun and two hostages if that was the vehicle that he had taken, and now he had to worry about the two other people in the car with Bear Darnell.

April heard the radio chatter as her units followed behind and from the units coming south on Route 7. She heard the Sheriff place a roadblock just south of their location, and she brought her GPS up to look at the route ahead. Sharon followed it up and said, "The area for the road block is going to be set up by the Hollis Country Store, and that's about twenty miles up the road. He should hit it soon."

April looked at her and said, "We're too far back. By the time we get there anything could happen." They had the light bar and siren on as they sped up, and April wondered if this was going to be a wild goose chase or not, then she thought about the people in the car. They had no idea what kind of monster they had in their car.

Darnell finally began to relax. He had eaten, had some cash, a car, a gun, and a couple of hostages. He began to look at the young woman in the front seat now and decided that what he needed to do now was to spend some time with her. What did he need her husband for when he could drive himself out now that he was pretty far up on Route 7. He leaned forward and told the husband to slow down, then he began to look for a road to turn off. About a quarter mile later he saw a sign for Little Bear Lake on the right, and he told the man to make the turn. He looked behind and did not see a car, and he felt that he had made the right decision.

The man seemed worried, but he obeyed and turned, not really knowing why he wanted to go to the lake. The road immediately changed from pavement to gravel, then the trees lined both sides of the road as the Toyota made its way down it. Darnell told him to go slow as he looked around. He wanted to be far enough away from the road so that no one would hear a gunshot, and he finally made them stop about fifty yards further. He pointed to a dirt road on the left and said, "Make that turn and head in til I say stop." The nervous husband turned, then he realized that they were in trouble and said, "Please mister. You have all of our money and car. Leave us here. There's no way we can get ahold of anyone for a long time. Please mister. Please don't hurt my wife." His wife stated crying now as she realized their predicament, then Darnell said, "Shut up and stop the car. Now, hand me the key."

Once he had the key fob he opened his door and got out as he told them to get out at the same time. He made the woman come to their side and began walking them into the woods, then stopped once they reached a tall pine tree. He grabbed the woman by the arm as he pointed the pistol at her husband's head, then he squeezed the trigger. At the sound of the pistol firing the woman watched her husband's body shoot forward and land on the ground. She tried to scream at that moment but the man had his hand around her mouth as he forced her to the ground. He pressed the pistol to the back of her head and said, "Shut up or I'll kill you!" He turned her over and back handed her hard, then he hit her several times in the side of her head until she laid still and did not fight him. He set his pistol on the ground next to her and began to rip her clothes off, then he took her.

She cried and tried to fight him off but he was much too strong. The shock of seeing her husband shot right before her eyes were too much and she began to go into shock herself, then the second that he finished raping her he placed his hands on her throat and began to squeeze it hard. He felt her hands on his arms as she tried to pull them away, then he saw the life leaving her as her body finally went limp. He was breathing hard now as he stood up and pulled his pants back up, then he looked at the two bodies on the ground, turned, and headed back to the car.

He sat a moment after starting the car to settle himself down, then he backed up and headed back to the paved road. Once he made the right turn and headed north, he felt real good about his situation. He had pleased himself with the woman, then made sure that she would not be a problem to him ever again. He nodded as he thought that he had made the mistake of trying to keep Amanda, and he had encountered nothing but trouble for that. From now on he would simply take what he wanted then kill the woman right away. He rolled the window down to take in some fresh air as he grabbed another bottle of water and took a long pull from it. A quick glance in the rearview mirror told him that he was far ahead of a car behind him, then he saw another one coming south.

He looked to make sure that it was not a cop car, then relaxed when he saw the blue F150 pass by him as he headed south, its driving waiving a hello to him. He felt that he maybe he was more worried than he needed to be. Up here in this area he would be lucky if her even spotted a cop. He relaxed and stuck his arm out of the window and picked up his speed some more. He was free.

The first patrol car to get close to him was still at least one mile back. The deputy had radioed his location and was told to hang back and wait for April to pass by. She wanted to stay close without letting the people in the Toyota know that they were being pursued. If Darnell was in the car, she did not want to endanger the other people with him, but she knew that at some point they were going to have to deal with that fact. Once Darnell hit the road block he would know that he was being followed, then he would see the deputies in front and behind him.

What he would do at that moment no one knew, but if he used the people as hostages it was going to turn into an entirely different situation for them all. She radioed the helicopter to hang back until Darnell approached the road block, then she sped up around any bends to make up time. She saw several cars coming south on Route 7 as they traveled north, and she asked Sharon how much farther now.

Sharon looked at the map on the laptop and traced along with her finger, then she said, "Maybe four, five miles, and he should see it. Depends how fast he's going and how far ahead he is of us." April looked at her, then Sharon said, "Like I just said, I have no idea at all." They both laughed and she pressed the accelerator harder then.

Chapter 22

The residents of the Hot Springs area kept glued to the television as they watched coverage of the escaped criminal. The local television station had their own helicopter in the air and it was on the way north on Route 7 as the news anchor said, "We know that a deputy that was escorting Bear Darnell was killed when his vehicle went off the side of Route 298 as it traveled east. He was headed to the prison when the accident occurred. Although we do not have all of the details of the crash we did learn that it happened on a sharp bend of the road. As you can see on your screens it appears that the patrol car rolled quite a ways at a high rate of speed before coming into contact with that large tree."

Viewers were stunned as they saw the horrific scene, then the news anchor said, "Bear Darnell, who was wanted for the kidnapping of young Amanda Webb, and the murders of Dolores Richards and the two sisters, Karen and Robin Potter, is believed to be armed and dangerous. Sheriff Thomas of the Garland Sheriff's Department wants everyone to stay at home. It is believed that Darnell stopped a passer-by on the highway and forced the driver of that vehicle to take him out of the area. Right now Channel Six has our Sky Cam helicopter in the air as it travels north on Route 7. The sheriff department believes that Darnell is travelling north in a red Toyota and is giving pursuit at this time. We will try to see if we can spot it, so be sure not to touch that dial."

In the usually quiet area of north Garland County residents were not used to seeing such drama play out on their screens, and there was no way anyone would change the dial on their televisions now.

Darnell was feeling pretty good right now as he felt the breeze blowing in his face. He slowed down and grabbed the cash to take a quick look and see how much he had. Having to keep his eyes on the road ahead, he figured that he had at least a hundred and maybe fifty bucks. Not bad. He could eat with that and find another source for cash later once he cleared the entire area. For now he knew that no one knew he had the car he was using, so as long as he didn't do anything stupid he was going to get out of the area soon enough. He pressed down on the accelerator to bring his speed back up to fifty, making sure that he would not take any risks at all.

April finally slowed as she made the last turn. They both saw a car up ahead and she slowed even more to maintain the wide gap between them. She did not want to arouse the occupants, and felt that, since she was driving an unmarked unit, she was OK to follow from where she was at. She called her patrol units and had them fall further back to be sure that they were not seen. Sharon said, "Any time now." Just then they heard a helicopter above them and looked at each other in surprise. April said, "I told them to stay back until I called them." She reached for her radio just as Sharon rolled her window down and looked up. She popped her head back in and said, "Just what we need. It's a news chopper."

April called Sheriff Thomas and told him what was happening, hoping that he could get them to fall back as Sharon began to waive her hands in the air at it. The last thing they needed was for Darnell to see or hear it, then he would panic and take off. Sheriff Thomas cussed, then told April he was getting on the horn with the TV station right away.

April watched as the chopper pulled ahead of them and headed towards the car in front of them, then she decided to speed up. Both she and Sharon were stunned to see the news helicopter go by them and hoped that the sheriff could get it stopped before they blew everything.

Darnell saw another car coming his way and leaned forward a bit. He relaxed as he saw that it was just another regular car, then he was about to remind himself to just chill when he heard a helicopter approaching. He looked in his rearview mirror but only saw a car still far enough back. It did appear closer than before, but he could not see the helicopter. He began to look around as he increased his speed, then he looked ahead and he saw two cars parked in the middle of the road and they were both facing him as they had their noses pointed at each other. He slammed his brakes and cursed as the helicopter now flew just above him. He stuck his head out of the window and saw that it had a large red number six painted on its side, and he knew that it was from the TV station.

He pounded his steering wheel and cursed again as he looked at the road block ahead one more time. Now he looked into the rearview mirror again and saw that the car that had been far behind him was real close, then he made out a whole line of police cars behind it. Now in a full panic mode, he screamed as he looked left and right, then he turned the car to his left, crossed the road, and sped into the tree line. He hit the tree line hard and fast and encountered heavy brush as the speed of the car pushed it deep into the brush, then it came to a stop.

He could not believe that this had happened. He grabbed the pistol and the bottle of water, then stuffed some cash into his pocket, opened his door, and fled into the forest as fast as he could. It was late in the day and would be dark in an hour or so, so if he was able to find a place to hide he would be able to get away in the dark. He ran and hit heavier brush, and, not really knowing what direction to take, he felt total fear as he tore through the brush. Branches slapped his face and he fell twice as he ran, then he felt the burn in his legs once again and cried out as he ran. He was breathing heavy and could feel the sweat running down his face as he ran, then he finally had to slow and catch his breath.

April could not believe what had just happened. Seeing the news helicopter begin to hover above the car they were behind let them know that it was the red Toyota, and after watching the car's reaction to it, they knew instantly that it was Bear

Darnell. Darnell had panicked when he heard the chopper above him, then he had come to a stop once he saw the road block ahead. She knew that they had let a few cars go past just to make it look normal to Darnell as he traveled towards them. They knew that the last vehicle they let pass was the only one that would be safe enough to go, then they closed the road, called in to report that they were ready, then waited.

She had sped up at that point, called the rest of her units to her, and told her department helicopter to get that news chopper out of the area. She and Sharon watched as Darnell made a sharp turn to his left, then crossed the road and headed straight for the wood line on his left. April sped up to catch up as the units behind her closed in, then they all saw the red Toyota disappear into the forest. She reached the area where it had gone into the woods moments later, then she and Sharon jumped out of the car.

April saw her department chopper get in front of the news helicopter and issue a warning for it to leave the area, then, as her deputies came to their side, she said, "We're going in. Keep sharp because he has a gun on him and is desperate." One of her deputies said, "I thought that there were others in the car with him but I didn't see anyone else come out." April said, "Check the car when we get to it, then join us if it's empty, let's go."

Ten deputies now joined April and Sharon as they ran into the gap created by the red Toyota with their weapons drawn. They tried to spread out some as they reached the car, then everyone saw it empty and continued their pursuit. They all knew that he was not too far ahead as the one deputy checked the trunk of the car for the owners before he too ran to join his team.

Darnell had to go again because he knew that the cops were too close. He had to stop a moment to catch his breath, and he took a few more big gulps of water before he started running again. The woods here were now beginning to spread out more, and the flatness of the terrain allowed him to make some good time as he ran at a fast pace. He dodged in and out of trees as he cut a path ahead, then he began to look for a good spot where he could hide at. As he ran with his eyes keyed on a set of thick trees to his right he hit a root on the ground and fell face first in the dirt. He let out a grunt as his face skidded on the forest floor, then he got up and took off again. He still had the pistol in his hand, but he had dropped what was left of his water not thinking about it at all as fear took over him.

He ran further and realized that he no longer had the water with him, but he saw the thick patch of trees and made his way to them.

April and Sharon saw broken branches and footsteps in the forest floor and were able to see easily the direction he had gone. They saw two places where it looked to them that he had taken a spill at, then they saw a patch of thick trees ahead and to their right and April gave the command to stop. They were all breathing heavy and sweating as they stopped and looked ahead, then April gave the command for them to kneel down so that they would not be seen. She lowered her voice and asked everyone to stay still and quiet, then she said, "He has to be worn out. I saw a bottle of water just about ten yards ahead, and it looked like he took a spill there also. He has to be panicking, tired, and winded, so I believe that he made it for that thick patch of trees ahead on the right."

They all looked and could see the water bottle on the ground, but only a few of the deputies that were close enough to April could make out the thick patch of trees ahead. As their breathing calmed some, April looked at her watch and said, "We don't have too much daylight left. If we don't get him in the next fifteen to thirty minutes at most it'll be dark and we will not be able to see him at all."

Special Agent Foster snuck up closer, then returned and said, "We need to send two people left and two right. Make your way as fast as possible around that thick patch and see if you can get behind him." April nodded and said, "We will give you all ten minutes before we go in from here. Be careful and remember that he's packing." Everyone knew what they had to do, then two of the deputies went right and two left as the rest of their group stayed put. April turned her radio off so that Darnell could not hear it, and she hoped that he would think they had gone another way as she and the rest of their team waited.

Chapter 23

Darnell remembered what had happened the last time that the cops had come after him. They had fooled him and came at him from all sides, and he had never suspected them to have crossed to the other side of the creek. Now that he had seen a lot of patrol cars coming his way, he knew that they were going to try to surround him again. This time he was not going to fall for it.

He rested a few moments as he tried to come up with a plan, then he backed up and started running again. If he stayed ahead of them they could not surround him. His legs felt like lead and his side hurt, but he knew that he had to make some space between he and them or it meant the end for him. He looked through the heavy canopy to see if he could see it turning gray out, but it was too hard to tell. Still, he knew that it was going to be dark soon. His idea to keep ahead was a great one, but he knew that there was no way he could pull it off too much longer.

He was way too exhausted now and was feeling thirsty again, so he decided to just find a good spot to hide and to stay low and quiet. He may be able to just remain out of sight until it got dark out, then he would be rested and be able to just walk away. Up ahead was a large boulder next to a pine tree, and he decided that it was good cover, so he started for it. He was winded but he felt that the cops had to be tired also. He would rest behind the boulder and just keep an eye out for them, then hope that they would not see him and that the blackness of night would envelope them all soon.

April nodded at Sharon that it was time, then they took off running towards the thick trees as they spread out. Surprised that they had not encountered any resistance, they reached the thicket at the same time as the four deputies came out from the left and right. Sharon cussed and said, "He must have figured us out from what we did to him back at the creek. He can't be that far ahead and he has to be tired, come on." They all followed Sharon as she took off.

Channel Six covered the entire event, showing its viewers the red Toyota smashing into the tree line, then showing the Sheriff Department chopper as it got to with a few feet of the news chopper and commanded them to leave. The news helicopter backed off at first, then, when the Sheriff chopper headed into the forest, they decided to hover above the area where the Toyota had gone into the forest. Channel Six news anchor Sophia Kerner told their viewers all about Bear Darnell as all of this had taken place, as well as describing the area where this event was taking place and now, as the chopper camera showed the car in the woods, she said, "At this very moment Garland County deputies are in that very forest giving chase. They need to capture Darnell before it gets too dark out and he has a chance to escape. And now joining us to offer his experience in this is former police lieutenant John Pierce, John?"

As the viewers were getting their fill of the situation, April split to Sharon's left and took half of the deputies as the rest followed the FBI agent. They all saw that the trees were very spread out in front of them and were able to see if Darnell would be by any of those trees as they spread out. With weapons at the ready, they all advanced and saw the large boulder ahead. They felt certain that he had to have taken refuge by it since it provided great protection for him.

As they knelt and got behind cover, April made the decision to move a bit further ahead to one of the large trees. Just as she reached it, a shot rang out and hit the branch just inches from her face. She hit the ground as her team all began returning fire. For the next minute it seemed like an old west gunfight as bullets were traded between the law officers and Darnell, then everything went quiet suddenly.

During the firing, only Special Agent Foster had begun to count the number of rounds that Darnell had fired at them. She knew that he had taken one of the deputy's Glock 9 mm. and

she knew that it had a fifteen round magazine. She laid behind
one of the trees returning fire, then she reloaded just as the firing ceased. She had counted ten shots coming from him, then
thought that there were supposed to be two people in the car
with him. If he shot them both he should have three bullets left.
It was possible that he still had five more, but either way, he was
almost out of ammo.

She yelled out, "April, when he took your deputy's pistol, did
he take any of his magazines?" April yelled back, not sure, let
me check." She looked at the large boulder ahead on more time,
knowing that her deputies would cover her, and she reached for
her mic and called in. It took a few minutes to confirm it, but
they let her know that the magazines on the deputy had been
accounted for, as well as his revolver that he had carried con-
cealed attached to his leg. April knew that Sharon had counted
his rounds as she had been trained to do, and she was glad to
have her along.

April called out, "None extra Sharon." Sharon thought a moment, then said aloud, "Five at most." Everyone there now
knew that Darnell was low on ammunition, but he still had five
rounds at most available. April made a decision, then she raised
her head and yelled out, "Darnell, there's no way you are getting
out of here. We have you surrounded now and we all have extra
magazines. What do you have left, five at the most? Throw the
gun out and come out with your hands up. Don't make us come
in and kill you Bear." She had decided to make it personal by
calling him by his first name, hoping that he would answer her
back.

For a moment, it was quiet. Then they heard him respond
from behind the boulder as he said, "There's no way I am going
to prison. I messed up before and let you grab me, but never
again. You see how dark it's getting now? In a few minutes you
won't be able to see me anymore. I'll take my chances and wait
a few more minutes." The second that April had spoken to him
she got up and ran straight to the opposite side of the boulder,
then she bent low as he spoke back. She was only a few feet

away now and he had no idea that she had come that close, then she looked to see which way was best for her to take before she made her move. Left, or right?

Just then she heard Sharon's voice as she said, "Right girl, right." Sharon wanted to distract Darnell so that April could surprise him, so she said, "How about a deal Darnell. I am FBI Special Agent Foster. Surrender and I will see to it that you only do six or seven years. You'll still be young when you get out, and may even get out earlier on good behavior." She knew that he had no chance of ever getting anything but a life sentence at the least, but she just wanted to distract him for a brief moment, and it worked.

Darnell laughed loudly at her and said, "I may fish for a living cop but I'm not stupid. He stood and fired two shots at them as April made it around the large boulder. Just as he fired his second shot she made it to his left side and yelled, "Drop it now!" Darnell jumped back as he was startled, then he made the mistake of raising his pistol at her as he jumped to his right. With only a second to make a decision, April had no choice but to open fire, and fired a three round burst. Since he had moved at that moment, only a single shot had caught him in the left arm. The jolt from the impact turned him sideways and caused his left hand to drop, then April dove into him. Her weight knocked him against the boulder, then she swung the butt of her pistol hard and caught him on the side of his head.

The large man dropped to the ground as April stepped on his right wrist where he was still holding the pistol. She yelled at him to drop it as she trained her pistol on him, then two of her deputies came from behind her. One held his pistol on Darnell and gave him commands to drop his pistol as the other one bent to grab it from his hand. A couple of anxious seconds later they had disarmed him, then they turned him over and placed handcuffs of his wrists. It was all over now.

He yelled out in pain as his arm was bent to his back, causing the bullet wound to hurt more, but the deputy that had taken his pistol away did a quick search on him for any additional weapons. They stood Darnell up and searched him again as the rest of the team arrived. Everyone there was breathing a bit heavy, but they all had smiles on their faces as Sharon looked at Darnell. She saw that April had taken a shot not to kill, and looked over at her. April said, "Yeah, I know I took a risk, but the couple whose car he took, we need to know what he did with them." Sharon read him his rights, then April turned her radio on and read him his rights over the air so that it was recorded by their body cameras and heard by the department.

They began their walk back as it was turning grey out, and April said, "I sure hope that one of you yucks know the way back because I don't want to have to spend the night out here." They all laughed as they headed back, glad that they had been fortunate enough to have captured him at the last minute. They all knew that if it had gotten dark out he would have been able to leave the area, then a large scale manhunt would have to take place in hopes of finding him.

Now that they had him in custody and an ambulance was called in, April told five of her officers there that she wanted them to follow the ambulance back to the hospital. There was no way she was going to allow Bear Darnell to escape them ever again. They asked him about the couple but he did not respond. Once her adrenaline had calmed down she called Sheriff Thomas to let him know the good news, then, as the team made its way out of the forest, the Channel Six helicopter still flying above turned its spotlight on them and all of the viewers saw that Darnell was in custody.

As the media began to tell its viewers their version of what had taken place, several of the media vans arrived at the scene. Detective Sanchez and Special Agent Foster told the reporters, "No comment." They were still not pleased that their interference had almost cost them the ability to capture Darnell, and each knew that Sheriff Thomas was going to deal with them severely. Both, April and Sharon watched as the paramedics began to treat Darnell's wound, then they watched as the ambulance began to head out with a police escort. Sharon high fived her new friend and said, "Come on, let's head to the hospital and speak with that scumbag. We need to find out what became of the two people in the car."

Chapter 24

The ER doctors treated Bear Darnell's wound as April and Special Agent Foster waited. Once he was moved out of surgery the doctor wanted him to rest since he had lost a lot of blood, and the two ladies took an opportunity to grab a cup of coffee in the hospital cafeteria as they coordinated with the crime scene unit who were now working on the red Toyota, gathering prints and DNA evidence. A search was underway for the couple who owned that vehicle, Gabe and Vanessa Harold, since the vehicle registration had been recovered.

Finally the time came when they could begin interrogating Darnell, so both officers passed by the guard they had posted at the door of the room and entered. Darnell had woken, found himself handcuffed to the bed, and saw them coming up to his bed, then he looked away and stared out of the window. No one said a word for a moment, then Darnell said, "I know what you want. I need a lawyer before I talk to you." April said, "Do you have your own attorney or do you want the court to appoint one for you?" He now turned to face them and said, "I can't afford one, so I want the court to appoint one for me." He turned away again, then April said, "That's fine Mr. Darnell, we will get to work on that for you. If you have any decency at all left in you why don't you at least tell us where the young couple that owned the Toyota are? They have families that deserve to know what happened to them."

Without looking at them, he said, "Lawyer. I don't trust you." The two women looked at each other now as Sharon said, "We will return once you have your attorney, but I want you to know that unless you give us the information we want, no attorney on Earth will be able to help you. Be smart and help yourself here." They started to leave the room when he said, "OK, but I want a lawyer. I want you to record this that I cooperated with you about that couple." They both agreed, then April said, "Go on."

He turned to face them again and said, "Off a road that takes you to Little Bear Lake. I can't remember the number of the road. Once you go in there is a dirt road on the left that you pass by. They're down there, dead. I won't say anymore til I see my lawyer, but remember that I cooperated with you." They thanked him and walked out as April called Sheriff Thomas. He told her that he would let the judge know that Darnell requested an attorney, and that he had cooperated with the law regarding the missing couple by telling them where he had left the young couple that owned the red Toyota. She told him that he had killed them both, and he said, "We are going to prosecute him to the fullest extent of the law. Just like he showed no mercy to his victims, we will show him no mercy either." April heard the anger in his voice and shared his feeling as they walked to her car.

April had her dispatcher send units to the road entrance for Little Bear Lake to start searching for the couple as she and Sharon made their way there. They wondered how he had killed them, then wondered if he had raped the woman. They would find that out an hour later how brutal he had been as they looked at the two bodies of Gabe and Vanessa Harold. Once they saw that Vanessa had been strangled after being raped, April said, "Had I known that he did this I would have killed him when I had the chance. He executed her husband, then beat the poor woman before raping her. He really is a monster." Sharon nodded because she too felt the same way.

Sharon, being an FBI agent, was not supposed to hear April say those words, but she was human too and also knew that she would have done the same thing. The crime scene van arrived and began their work in the dark as the two officers departed and headed back to the station. Again a media van passed by them on the gravel road as they rushed to the scene where the two bodies were. April shook her head as she watched it and said, "It seems that people now crave for the worst possible news that they can find. It makes me feel sad inside that we've come to this as a society."

The media covered the story of the escape, the capture, and the murder of the innocent couple as people once again were glued to their screens. They were not allowed to speak with Darnell and were kept away at the hospital, then he was transferred to the jail in Hot Springs once he was declared OK to travel the following day. His court appointed attorney had met with him at the hospital and advised him not to speak with anyone, including the media, without his presence.

He told him that, once he was transferred to the prison and booked in, he would meet with him to discuss his case further. Before he left the hospital room Bear stopped him and said, "Tell me the truth, what do you think the cops are going to do to me?" His attorney had listened to him explain how he had been able to escape, then how he had taken the lives of the young couple. His lack of ability to show remorse or empathy for his victims worried him because he knew that once a jury heard the evidence, it would take a miracle to save his client from a penalty of death. Attorney Michael Phillips lowered his voice first, then said, "Mr. Darnell, in 2013 the Arkansas General Assembly passed a new law instituting the death penalty in this state. They use lethal injection here, and although you cooperated with the law and told them where they could find the young couple, I need to tell you that this case is going to be very difficult to defend. I promise you that I will do my best to see that you do not receive the death penalty, but you need to prepare yourself for that possibility."

Darnell humphed loudly, then he said, "Maybe I need a new lawyer. It sounds to me that you don't have what it takes to fight for me." Attorney Phillips nodded at him and said, "That certainly is your prerogative, but no matter who you get to represent you, they will need to face the same charges that the FBI and the Garland County Sheriff Department will bring against you. Please understand Mr. Darnell, the fact is that they have a mound of evidence against you. You have now added more charges upon yourself since your escape from the law. We need to discuss how to best approach this matter. Even if you enter a plea of insanity you will need to be tested and hope that the phycologists find in your favor."

He asked Darnell if he still wanted him to represent him, then he left the room after explaining to him what the next steps he would face were going to be, promising to meet him in the jail after he was booked in. Darnell laid in his bed thinking about his case. He had never thought about the possibility of having to face the death penalty, and now tears began to flow as he turned to face the window once again.

The following day Darnell was transferred to prison and booked in, then he met with his lawyer for several hours before having to go through the interrogation process with Special Agent Foster and Detective Sanchez. With the guidance of his attorney, he explained how the accident had taken place while he was being transferred to prison, then how he had managed to stop the young Harold couple, Gabe and Vanessa.

His attorney used that moment to try to explain that, as a result of the accident, his client was not thinking clearly and only thought about getting away from there to seek medical attention. Mr. Darnell says that he was offered a ride by the young couple once they arrived at the scene of the accident. April looked at Darnell and said, "Yet you were in a clear state of mind to remove my deputy's weapon from him. As far as being offered a ride, we need to ask then why it was that they did not drive you to the hospital? How was it that you ended up traveling in the opposite direction. The receipt we found in the car showed that you all stopped for snacks before proceeding farther away from the hospital. We have a witness putting you in the back seat of the car as it drove away from a gas station. Then Mr. Darnell, you took the couple to a remote location where you executed Gabe Harold, then proceeded to beat and rape Vanessa Harold before you strangled her to death. You strangled her so hard that you crushed her trachea."

She turned to attorney Phillips and said, "Is that the right state of mind that you referred to counselor?" Sharon knew that they had just nailed Darnell to a cross, then she stood and said, "We will be speaking again once we present all the charges to your client." Darnell said, "Just a second. I want to explain my side here. The guy attacked me once they drove me out to that remote spot. I had no choice but to defend myself. His old lady came at me trying to help him kill me, so I had to fight her off too."

Again he showed no signs of remorse as he explained how he had murdered Gabe Harold by a single shot to the back of the head, then proceeded to brutally rape, and strangle Vanessa Harold to death. His grip on her throat had been so hard and forceful, that it had crushed her trachea, but he claimed that he had to fight for his own life at that moment and was not responsible for his actions. He could not explain how he had shot the husband in the back of the head instead of his chest. He did not seem to care when Detective Sanchez informed him of the fact that he had raped Vanessa Harold, and his attorney sighed as he pictured a jury listening to all of the testimony and to the DA telling them that Darnell never showed any signs of empathy or remorse to his victims.

Once the two law enforcement officers had all of the information they needed, they ended the interrogation and told Attorney Phillips that he would need to be present once more charges were brought against his client. Just as they both stood to leave the small room Darnell looked over at his lawyer and saw him gathering a stack of papers, then he blurted out, "Hey, just a minute here. I have not heard anything about cutting me a deal here."

Special Agent Foster said, "That is correct Mr. Darnell, and that is up to the District Attorney, not us. All that we can do is to recommend what we feel is the proper justice here. Any deals discussed on your behalf will be discussed between your attorney and the DA's office. As far as we are concerned here, we are going to ask for the death penalty for you." The two officers then departed the room as Darnell began to shout at his attorney. Ten minutes later Attorney Phillips left the room, and he was no longer representing Bear Darnell.

Chapter 25

The trial date was postponed for three more weeks to allow the defendant to heal from his wound, then the chaos of people and the media surrounded the courthouse as jury selection began. One week later the jury had been selected and a date set for the trial itself to begin.

The new attorney representing Bear Darnell asked the court for more time to better prepare but his request was denied. He had gone over all of the charges against his client and had studied the mounds of evidence against his client, and he knew that he was not going to win the case. He had no chance, especially after having his client tested by psychologists to see if he was sane to stand trial. Bear Darnell was declared sane, and the trial began the following day.

The media was allowed to record it, but due to the Covid-19 epidemic, only family members were allowed inside the courtroom itself. The judge ordered that the jurors were not to be shown on camera, then he gave the jury their instructions just before the trial proceeded. Both the DA and the defense presented their sides of the case, and Darnell, who had pleaded innocent, sat in the courtroom watching and listening to the proceedings, often glaring at the jurors. His attorney had to stop to give him advice several times when he reacted to Amanda Webb's testimony as the jury members watched with keen interest each day. The media coverage played it all out on the television screen and everyone saw how despicable a human being Bear Darnell was. Not one single person felt sorry for him.

Panel members that the news station had covering the trial added their comments nightly and during the trial on what their thoughts were concerning the case, and never once did they agree that the defense had made a valid point on behalf of their client. Because he knew that it would not fare well for his client if he were to take the stand, he strongly advised him not to. Darnell finally took his advice, and they proceeded to closing arguments. It took only two weeks for the trial to come to an end, then the judge sequestered the jury, gave them final instructions, and declared the trial ready for jury deliberation. To the total surprise of everyone involved in the case and watching the case, it took jury members only two hours to come to a final verdict.

The judge had not granted Bear Darnell bail, so he had been incarcerated during the trial proceedings, and he was escorted back into the courtroom before the jury was called back in. Once again the judge gave both sides further instructions, then a choice for sentencing was presented to Darnell if he was found guilty. He took the advice of his counsel and chose to have the judge administer the sentencing, still believing that the jury had to believe his side of the story. He began to believe it himself as the trial proceeded.

The attorney was hopeful as they filed back so soon after deliberation because the shorter the deliberation time usually meant that an acquittal followed. The judge called the jury back, then covered more instructions and some questions from the attorneys, then he was presented the verdict. All eyes were on the judge as everyone waited to hear the verdict, not a sound could be heard, and the camera showed Darnell looking back at Amanda Webb just before the judge read the verdict.

Judge Amos went through each charge against Bear Darnell, declaring him guilty each time, then Darnell stood up and began cussing at him and at the jury. Deputies restrained him and the judge ordered that he be gagged, then, as two deputies held him down on his chair, Judge Amos announced a date for sentencing, which was to be three weeks from that date. Everyone watched as Bear Darnell was escorted out of the room as he fought against the deputies, and they heard the muffled sounds coming from his gag as he screamed insults at everyone in the courtroom.

Family members cried as the verdict was read, and although they now had received justice for their loved ones, they were all saddened knowing that they would never be able to have them in their lives anymore. All the panel members from the television station agreed with the jury verdict, as well as everyone watching at home.

It took Amanda a short time to get back to a normal routine, but she felt bad for the families of the people Darnell had murdered. She knew how fortunate she had been to have escaped. Special Agent Foster resumed her duties at the Bureau, and Detective April Sanchez received a commendation for her work on the case. Everyone who had watched the trial or had been involved with it had agreed with the decision of the jury, and were all present three weeks later for the sentencing trial as they were glued to their screens once again.

No one was surprised when Judge Amos handed Bear Darnell the death penalty by lethal injection, and Darnell ended up having to be restrained and gagged once again. He never apologized to the families of his victims and never showed remorse for his actions, and six months later he was put to death by the State of Arkansas as family members attended. His last words were that everyone was wrong and that he was innocent. He never acknowledged the fact that he was a monster.

If you enjoyed reading this book please take a moment to rate it, it would be appreciated it very much. All of my novels are available on Goodreads and on Amazon. It is really sad that we have people committing evil acts in our world. Please remember to always be vigilant and aware of your surroundings.

ABOUT THE AUTHOR

J.L. Lara lives in Florida with his wife. He is a U S Army veteran, is retired, and enjoys spending time with his family, especially his grandson. He loves to read, garden, and his hobby of model trains. Thank you for reading this book.

[CL1]Y

[CL1]Y

www.ingramcontent.com/pod-product-compliance
Lightning Source LLC
Chambersburg PA
CBHW072229150726
48002CB00005B/2000